PRAISE FOR STEPHEN KING

'The most remarkable storyteller in modern American literature'
– Mark Lawson, *Guardian*

'A writer of excellence . . . King is one of the most fertile story-tellers of the modern novel' – *The Sunday Times*

'King has inspired a whole generation to read. He's made them read good, witty prose . . . a fabulous teller of stories who can create an entire new world and make the reader live in it'
– *Express*

'Stephen King's novels are, among other things, great examples of time-capsule prose. They capture the pop culture texture of each American decade as beautifully as, say, *Close Encounters of the Third Kind* or *ET*' – Toby Litt, *The Times*

ABOUT THE AUTHOR

STEPHEN KING. Photograph © Shane Leonard

There is a reason why Stephen King is one of the bestselling writers in the world, *ever*. Described in the *Guardian* as an 'incredibly gifted writer' and in *The Sunday Times* as 'a writer of excellence', Stephen King writes stories that draw you in and are *impossible to put down*.

King is the author of more than sixty books, all of them worldwide bestsellers including the popular classics *Lisey's Story, Misery* and *The Institute*.

Many of his books and novellas have been turned into celebrated films, television series and streamed events, including *Doctor Sleep, Stand By Me* and *The Shawshank Redemption*.

King was the recipient of the 2003 National Book Foundation Medal for Distinguished Contribution to American Letters, in 2007 he won the Grand Master Award from the Mystery Writers of America and in 2015 received America's National Medal of Arts. He lives with his wife, Tabitha King, in Maine.

By Stephen King and published by Hodder & Stoughton

STEPHEN
KING
ELEVATION

HODDER

A CIP catalogue record for this title is available from the British Library

Paperback ISBN 978 1 473 69153 7
eBook ISBN 978 1 473 69154 4

Illustrations copyright © 2018 Mark Edward Geyer

Typeset in Bembo by Palimpsest Book Production Limited,
Falkirk, Stirlingshire

Printed and bound in Great Britain by Clays Ltd, Elcograf S.p.A.

Hodder & Stoughton policy is to use papers that are natural, renewable and
recyclable products and made from wood grown in sustainable forests.
The logging and manufacturing processes are expected to conform
to the environmental regulations of the country of origin.

Hodder & Stoughton Ltd
Carmelite House
50 Victoria Embankment
London EC4Y 0DZ

www.hodder.co.uk

Thinking of
Richard Matheson

Contents

ELEVATION

CHAPTER 1

Losing Weight

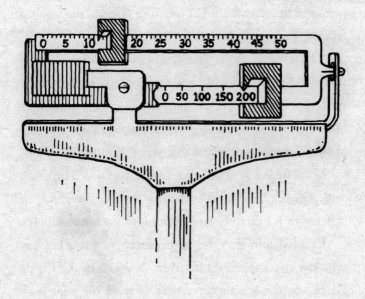

SCOTT CAREY KNOCKED ON the door of the Ellis condo unit, and Bob Ellis (everyone in Highland Acres still called him Doctor Bob, although he was five years retired) let him in. 'Well, Scott, here you are. Ten on the dot. Now what can I do for you?'

Scott was a big man, six-feet-four in his stocking feet, with a bit of a belly growing in front. 'I'm not sure. Probably nothing, but . . . I have a problem. I hope not a big one, but it might be.'

'One you don't want to talk to your regular doctor about?' Ellis was seventy-four, with thinning silver hair and a small limp that didn't slow him down much on the tennis court. Which was where he and Scott had met, and become friends. Not close friends, maybe, but friends, sure enough.

'Oh, I went,' Scott said, 'and got a checkup. Which was overdue. Bloodwork, urine, prostate, the whole nine yards. Everything checked out. Cholesterol a little high, but still in the normal range. It was diabetes I was worried about. WebMD suggested that was the most likely.'

Until he knew about the clothes, that was. The thing with the clothes wasn't on any website, medical or otherwise. It certainly had nothing to do with diabetes.

Ellis led him into the living room, where a big bay window overlooked the fourteenth green of the Castle Rock gated community where he and his wife now lived. Doctor Bob played the occasional round, but mostly stuck to tennis. It was Ellis's wife who enjoyed golf, and Scott suspected that was the reason they were living here, when they weren't spending winters in a similar sports-oriented development in Florida.

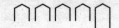

Ellis said, 'If you're looking for Myra, she's at her Methodist Women's group. I think that's right, although it might be one of her town committees. Tomorrow she's off to Portland for a meeting of the New England Mycological Society. That woman hops around like a hen on a hot griddle. Take off your coat, sit down, and tell me what's on your mind.'

Although it was early October and not particularly cold, Scott was wearing a North Face parka. When he took it off and laid it beside him on the sofa, the pockets jingled.

'Would you like coffee? Tea? I think there's a break-fast pastry, if—'

'I'm losing weight,' Scott said abruptly. 'That's what's on my mind. It's sort of funny, you know. I used to steer clear of the bathroom scale, because these last ten years or so, I haven't been crazy about the news I got from it. Now I'm on it first thing every morning.'

Ellis nodded. 'I see.'

No reason for *him* to avoid the bathroom scale, Scott thought; the man was what his grandmother would have called a stuffed string. He'd probably live another twenty years, if a wild card didn't come out of the deck. Maybe even make the century.

'I certainly understand the scale-avoidance syndrome, saw it all the time when I was practicing. I also saw

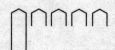

the opposite, compulsive weighing. Usually in bulimics and anorexics. You hardly look like one of those.' He leaned forward, hands clasped between his skinny thighs. 'You *do* understand that I'm retired, don't you? I can advise, but I can't prescribe. And my advice will probably be for you to go back to your regular doctor, and make a full disclosure.'

Scott smiled. 'I suspect my doc would want me in the hospital for tests right away, and last month I landed a big job, designing interlocking websites for a department store chain. I won't go into details, but it's a plum. I was very fortunate to get the gig. It's a large step up for me, and I can do it without moving out of Castle Rock. That's the beauty of the computer age.'

'But you can't work if you fall ill,' Ellis said. 'You're a smart guy, Scott, and I'm sure you know that weight-loss isn't just a marker for diabetes, it's a marker for cancer. Among other things. How much weight are we talking about?'

'Twenty-eight pounds.' Scott looked out the window and observed white golf carts moving over green grass beneath a blue sky. As a photograph, it would have looked good on the Highland Acres website. He was sure they had one – everyone did these days, even roadside stands selling corn and apples had websites – but he hadn't created it. He had moved on to bigger things. 'So far.'

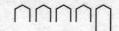

Bob Ellis grinned, showing teeth that were still his own. 'That's a fair amount, all right, but my guess is you could stand to lose it. You move very well on the tennis court for a big man, and you put in your time on the machines in the health club, but carrying too many pounds puts a strain not just on the heart but the whole kit and caboodle. As I'm sure you know. From WebMD.' He rolled his eyes at this, and Scott smiled. 'What are you now?'

'Guess,' Scott said.

Bob laughed. 'What do you think this is, the county fair? I'm fresh out of Kewpie dolls.'

'You were in general practice for what, thirty-five years?'

'Forty-two.'

'So don't be modest, you've weighed thousands of patients thousands of times.' Scott stood up, a tall man with a big frame wearing jeans, a flannel shirt, and scuffed-up Georgia Giants. He looked more like a woodsman or a horse-wrangler than a web designer. 'Guess my weight. We'll get to my fate later.'

Doctor Bob cast the eye of a professional up and down Scott Carey's seventy-six inches – more like seventy-eight, in the boots. He paid particular attention to the curve of belly over the belt, and the long thigh muscles built up by leg-presses and hack squats on

5

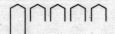

machines Doctor Bob now avoided. 'Unbutton your shirt and hold it open.'

Scott did this, revealing a gray tee with UNIVERSITY OF MAINE ATHLETIC DEPARTMENT on the front. Bob saw a broad chest, muscular, but developing those adipose deposits wiseass kids liked to call man-tits.

'I'm going to say . . .' Ellis paused, interested in the challenge now. 'I'm going to say 235. Maybe 240. Which means you must have been up around 270 before you started to lose. I must say you carried it well on the tennis court. That much I wouldn't have guessed.'

Scott remembered how happy he had been when he'd finally mustered the courage to get on the scale earlier this month. Delighted, actually. The steady rate of the weight-loss since then was worrisome, yes, but only a little. It was the clothes thing that had changed worry to fright. You didn't need WebMD to tell you that the clothes thing was more than strange; it was fucking outré.

Outside, a golf cart trundled past. In it were two middle-aged men, one in pink pants, one in green, both overweight. Scott thought they would have done themselves some good by ditching the cart and walking their round, instead.

'Scott?' Doctor Bob said. 'Are you there, or did I lose you?'

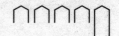

'I'm here,' Scott said. 'The last time we played tennis, I *did* go 240. I know, because that was when I finally got on the scale. I decided the time had come to drop a few pounds. I was starting to get all out of breath by the third set. But as of this morning, I weigh 212.'

He sat down again next to his parka (which gave another jingle). Bob eyed him carefully. 'You don't look like 212 to me, Scott. Pardon me for saying, but you look quite a bit heavier than that.'

'But healthy?'

'Yes.'

'Not sick.'

'No. Not to look at you, anyway, but—'

'Have you got a scale? I bet you do. Let's check it out.'

Doctor Bob considered him for a moment, wondering if Scott's actual problem might be in the gray matter above his eyebrows. In his experience, it was mostly women who tended to be neurotic about their weight, but it happened with men, too. 'All right, let's do that. Follow me.'

Bob led him into a study stocked with bookshelves. There was a framed anatomy chart on one wall and a line of diplomas on another. Scott was staring at the paperweight between Ellis's computer and his printer.

Bob followed his gaze and laughed. He picked the skull up off the desk and tossed it to Scott.

'Plastic rather than bone, so don't worry about dropping it. A gift from my eldest grandson. He's thirteen, which I think of as the Age of Tasteless Gifts. Step over here, and let's see what we've got.'

In the corner was a gantry-like scale upon which two weights, one big and one little, could be moved until the steel beam balanced. Ellis gave it a pat. 'The only things I kept when I closed my office downtown were the anatomy chart on the wall and this. It's a Seca, the finest medical scale ever made. A gift from my wife, many years ago, and believe me when I say no one ever accused *her* of being tasteless. Or cheap.'

'Is it accurate?'

'Let's just say if I weighed a twenty-five-pound bag of flour on it, and the scale said it weighed twenty-four, I'd go back to Hannaford's and demand a refund. You should take off your boots if you want something close to a true weight. And why did you bring your coat?'

'You'll see.' Scott didn't take off his boots but put the parka on instead, to the tune of more jingling from the pockets. Now not just fully dressed but dressed for the outside on a day much colder than this one, he stepped on the scale. 'Let 'er rip.'

In order to allow for the boots and the coat, Bob

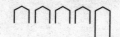

ran the counterweight all the way to 250, then worked backward, first sliding the weight, then nudging it along. The needle of the balance bar remained grounded at 240, and 230, and 220, which Doctor Bob would have thought impossible. Never mind the coat and boots; Scott Carey simply looked heavier than that. He could have been off in his estimate by a few pounds, but he had weighed too many overweight men and women to be *this* far off.

The bar balanced at 212 pounds.

'I'll be dipped in pitch,' Doctor Bob said. 'I need to have this thing recalibrated.'

'Don't think so,' Scott said. He stepped off the scale and put his hands in his coat pockets. From each, he took a fistful of quarters. 'Been saving these in an antique chamber pot for years. By the time Nora left, it was almost full. I must have five pounds of metal in each pocket, maybe more.'

Ellis said nothing. He was speechless.

'Now do you see why I didn't want to go to Dr Adams?' Scott let the coins slide back into his coat pockets with another jolly jingle.

Ellis found his voice. 'Let me be sure I have this right – you're getting the same weight at home?'

'To the pound. My scale's an Ozeri step-on, maybe not as good as this baby, but I've tested it and it's

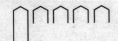

accurate. Now watch this. I usually like a little bump-and-grind music when I strip, but since we've undressed together in the club locker room, I guess I can do without it.'

Scott took off his parka and hung it on the back of a chair. Then, balancing with first one hand and then the other on Doctor Bob's desk, he took off his boots. Next came the flannel shirt. He unbuckled his belt, stepped out of his jeans, and stood there in his boxers, tee-shirt, and socks.

'I could shuck these as well,' he said, 'but I think I've taken off enough to make the point. Because, see, this is what scared me. The thing about the clothes. It's why I wanted to talk to a friend who could keep his mouth shut instead of my regular doc.' He pointed to the clothes and boots on the floor, then at the parka with its sagging pockets. 'How much would you say all that stuff weighs?'

'With the coins? At least fourteen pounds. Possibly as much as eighteen. Do you want to weigh them?'

'No,' Scott said.

He got back on the scale. There was no need to move the weights. The beam balanced at 212 pounds.

Scott dressed and they went back to the living room. Doctor Bob poured them each a tiny knock of

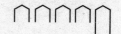

Woodford Reserve, and although it was only ten in the morning, Scott did not refuse. He took his down in a single swallow, and the whiskey lit a comforting fire in his stomach. Ellis took two delicate birdy sips, as if testing the quality, then tossed off the rest. 'It's impossible, you know,' he said as he put the empty glass on an endtable.

Scott nodded. 'Another reason I didn't want to talk to Dr Adams.'

'Because it would be in the system,' Ellis said. 'A matter of record. And yes, he'd have insisted you undergo tests in order to find out exactly what's going on with you.'

Although he didn't say so, Scott thought *insisted* was too mild. In Dr Adams's consulting room, the phrase that had popped into his head was *taken into custody*. That was when he'd decided to keep his mouth shut and talk to his retired medical friend instead.

'You *look* 240,' Ellis said. 'Is that how you feel?'

'Not exactly. I felt a little . . . mmm . . . *ploddy* when I actually did weigh 240. I guess that's not a real word, but it's the best I can do.'

'I think it's a good word,' Ellis said, 'whether it's in the dictionary or not.'

'It wasn't just being overweight, although I knew I was. It was that, and age, and . . .'

'The divorce?' Ellis asked it gently, in his most Doctor Bobly way.

Scott sighed. 'Sure, that too. It's cast a shadow over my life. It's better now, *I'm* better, but it's still there. Can't lie about that. Physically, though, I never felt bad, still worked out a little three times a week, never got out of breath until the third set, but just . . . you know, ploddy. Now I don't, or at least not so much.'

'More energy.'

Scott considered, then shook his head. 'Not exactly. It's more like the energy I have goes further.'

'No lethargy? No fatigue?'

'No.'

'No loss of appetite?'

'I eat like a horse.'

'One more question, and you'll pardon me, but I have to ask.'

'Ask away. Anything.'

'There's no way this is a practical joke, right? Pulling the leg of the old retired sawbones?'

'Absolutely not,' Scott said. 'I guess I don't have to ask if you've ever seen a similar case, but have you ever read about one?'

Ellis shook his head. 'Like you, it's the clothes that I keep coming back to. And the quarters in your coat pockets.'

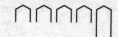

Join the club, Scott thought.

'No one weighs the same naked as they do dressed. It's as much a given as gravity.'

'Are there medical websites you can go on to see if there are any other cases like mine? Even ones that are sort of similar?'

'I can and will, but I can tell you now there won't be.' Ellis hesitated. 'This isn't just outside my experience, I'd say it's outside *human* experience. Hell, I want to say it's impossible. If, that is, your scale and mine weigh true, and I have no reason to believe otherwise. What happened to you, Scott? What was the genesis? Did you . . . I don't know, get irradiated by something? Maybe get a lungful of some off-brand bug-spray? Think.'

'I *have* thought. So far as I can tell, there's nothing. But one thing's for sure, I feel better having talked to you. Not just sitting on it.' Scott stood up and grabbed his jacket.

'Where are you going?'

'Home. I've got those websites to work on. It's a big deal. Although I have to tell you, it doesn't seem quite as big as it did.'

Ellis walked with him to the door. 'You say you've noted a steady weight-loss. Slow but steady.'

'That's right. A pound or so a day.'

13

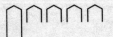

'No matter how much you eat.'

'Yes,' Scott said. 'And what if it continues?'

'It won't.'

'How can you be sure? If it's outside of human experience?'

To this Doctor Bob had no answer.

'Keep your mouth shut about this, Bob. Please.'

'I will if you promise to keep me informed. I'm concerned.'

'That I can do.'

On the stoop, they stood side by side, looking at the day. It was a nice one. Foliage was nearing peak, and the hills were burning with color. 'Moving from the sublime to the ridiculous,' Doctor Bob said, 'how are you doing with the restaurant ladies up the street from you? Heard you were having some problems there.'

Scott didn't bother asking Ellis where he had heard this; Castle Rock was a small town, and word got around. It got around faster, he supposed, when a retired doctor's wife was on all sorts of town and church committees. 'If Ms McComb and Ms Donaldson heard you calling them ladies, you'd be in their black books. And given my current problem, they're not even on my radar.'

An hour later Scott sat in his own study, part of a handsome three-decker on Castle View, above the town

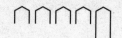

proper. A pricier address than he had been comfortable with, but Nora had wanted it, and he had wanted Nora. Now she was in Arizona and he was left with a place that had been too big even when it had been the two of them. Plus the cat, of course. He had an idea she had found it harder to leave Bill than to leave him. Scott recognized that was a little bitchy, but how often the truth was.

In the center of his computer screen, in big letters, were the words HOCHSCHILD-KOHN DRAFT SITE 4 MATERIAL. Hochschild-Kohn wasn't the chain he was working for, had been out of business for nearly forty years, but with a job as big as this one, it didn't hurt to be mindful of hackers. Hence the pseudonym.

When Scott double-clicked, a picture of an old-timey Hochschild-Kohn department store appeared (eventually to be replaced by a much more modern building, belonging to the actual company that had hired him). Below this: *You bring the inspiration, we bring the rest*.

It was this tossed-off tagline that had actually gotten him the job. Design skills were one thing; inspiration and clever sloganeering were another; when they came together, you had something special. *He* was special, this was his chance to prove it, and he intended to

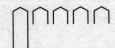

make the most of it. Eventually he would be working with an ad agency, he understood that, and they would tinker with his lines and graphics, but he thought that slogan would stay. Most of his basic ideas would also stay. They were strong enough to survive a bunch of New York City hotshots.

He double-clicked again, and a living room appeared on the screen. It was totally empty; there weren't even light fixtures. Outside the window was a greensward that just happened to be part of the Highland Acres golf course, where Myra Ellis had played many rounds. On a few occasions, Myra's foursome had included Scott's own ex-wife, who was now living (and presumably golfing) in Flagstaff.

Bill D. Cat came in, gave a sleepy miaow, and rubbed along his leg.

'Food soon,' Scott murmured. 'Few more minutes.' As though a cat had any concept of minutes in particular, or time in general.

As if I do, Scott thought. Time is invisible. Unlike weight.

Ah, but maybe that wasn't true. You could feel weight, yes – when you were carrying too much, it made you *ploddy* – but wasn't it, like time, basically just a human construct? Hands on a clock, numbers on a bathroom scale, weren't they only ways of trying to

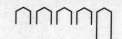

measure invisible forces that had visible effects? A feeble effort to corral some greater reality beyond what mere humans thought of as reality?

'Let it go, you'll drive yourself bugshit.'

Bill gave another miaow, and Scott returned his attention to the computer screen.

Above the barren living room was a search field containing the words *Pick Your Style!* Scott typed in *Early American*, and the screen came to life, not all at once, but slowly, as if each piece of furniture were being picked out by a careful shopper and added to the whole: chairs, a sofa, pink walls that were stenciled rather than papered, a Seth Thomas clock, a goodwife rag rug on the floor. A fireplace with a small cozy blaze within. The overhead fixture held hurricane lamps on wooden spokes. Those were a little over the top for Scott's taste, but the salespeople he was dealing with loved them, and assured Scott that potential customers would, too.

He could swipe and furnish a parlor, a bedroom, a study, all in Early American. Or he could return to the search field and furnish those virtual-reality rooms in Colonial, Garrison, Craftsman, or Cottage style. Today's job, however, was Queen Anne. Scott opened his laptop and began picking out display furniture.

Forty-five minutes later, Bill was back, rubbing and miaowing more insistently.

'Okay, okay,' Scott said, and got up. He went into the kitchen, Bill D. Cat leading the way with his tail up. There was a feline spring in Bill's step, and Scott was damned if he didn't feel pretty springy himself.

He dumped Friskies into Bill's bowl, and while the cat chowed down, he went out on the front porch for a breath of fresh air before going back to Selby wing chairs, Winfrey settees, Houzz highboys, all with the famous Queen Anne legs. He thought it was the kind of furniture you saw in funeral parlors, heavy shit trying to seem light, but different strokes for different folks.

He was in time to see 'the ladies,' as Doctor Bob had called them, coming out of their driveway and turning onto View Drive, long legs flashing beneath tiny shorts – blue for Deirdre McComb, red for Missy Donaldson. They were wearing identical tee-shirts advertising the restaurant they ran downtown on Carbine Street. Following them were their nearly identical boxers, Dum and Dee.

What Doctor Bob had said as Scott was leaving (probably wanting no more than to end their meeting on a lighter note) now recurred, something about Scott having a little trouble with the restaurant ladies. Which he was. Not a bitter relationship problem, or a mysterious weight-loss problem; more like a cold sore that wouldn't go away. Deirdre was the really annoying one,

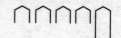

always with her faintly superior smile – the one that seemed to say *lord help me to bear these fools*.

Scott made a sudden decision and hustled back to his study (taking a nimble leap over Bill, who was reclining in the hall) and grabbed his tablet. Running back to the porch, he opened the camera app.

The porch was screened, which made him hard to see, and the women weren't paying any attention to him, anyway. They ran along the packed dirt shoulder on the far side of the Drive with their bright white sneakers scissoring and their ponytails swinging. The dogs, stocky but still young and plenty athletic, pounded along behind.

Scott had visited their home twice on the subject of those dogs, had spoken to Deirdre both times, and had borne that faintly superior smile patiently as she told him she really doubted that their dogs were doing their business on his lawn. Their backyard was fenced, she said, and in the hour or so each day when they were out ('Dee and Dum always accompany Missy and me on our daily runs') they were *very* well-behaved.

'I think they must smell my cat,' Scott had said. 'It's a territorial thing. I get that, and I understand you not wanting to leash them when you run, but I'd appreciate you checking out my lawn when you come back, and policing it up if necessary.'

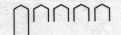

'*Policing*,' Deirdre had said, her smile never wavering. 'Seems a bit militaristic, but maybe that's just me.'

'Whatever you want to call it.'

'Mr Carey, dogs may be, as you say, *doing their business* on your lawn, but they're not *our* dogs. Perhaps it's something else that's concerning you? It wouldn't be a prejudice against same-sex marriage, would it?'

Scott had almost laughed, which would have been bad — even Trumpian — diplomacy. 'Not at all. It's a prejudice against not wanting to step in a surprise package left by one of your boxers.'

'Good discussion,' she had said, still with that smile (not maddening, as she might have hoped, but definitely irritating), and closed the door gently but firmly in his face.

With his mysterious weight-loss the farthest thing from his mind for the first time in days, Scott watched the two women running toward him with their dogs loping gamely along in their wake. Deirdre and Missy were talking as they ran, laughing about something. Their flushed cheeks shone with sweat and good health. The McComb woman was clearly the better runner of the two, and just as clearly holding back a bit to stay with her partner. They were paying zero attention to the dogs, which was hardly neglect; View Drive wasn't a hotbed of traffic, especially in the middle of the day. And Scott

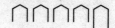
had to admit that the dogs were good about keeping out of the road. In that, at least, they were well-trained.

Not going to happen today, he thought. It never does when you're prepared. Yet it would be pleasant to wipe that little quirk of a smile off Ms McComb's—

But it did happen. First one of the boxers swerved, then the other followed. Dee and Dum ran onto Scott's lawn and squatted side by side. Scott raised his tablet and snapped three quick photos.

That evening, after an early supper of spaghetti carbonara followed by a wedge of chocolate cheesecake, Scott got on his Ozeri scale, hoping as he always did these days that things had finally started going the right way. They had not. In spite of the big meal he had just put away, the Ozeri informed him that he was down to 210.8 pounds.

Bill was watching him from the closed toilet seat, his tail curled neatly around his paws. 'Well,' Scott told him, 'it is what it is, right? As Nora used to say when she came home from those meetings of hers, life is what we make it and acceptance is the key to all our affairs.'

Bill yawned.

'But we also change the things we can, don't we? You hold the fort. I'm going to pay a visit.'

He grabbed his iPad and jogged the quarter mile to the renovated farmhouse where McComb and Donaldson had lived for the last eight months or so, since opening Holy Frijole. He knew their schedule pretty well, in the offhand way one gets to know one's neighbors' comings and goings, and this would be a good time to catch Deirdre alone. Missy was the chef at the restaurant, and usually left to start dinner prep around three. Deirdre, who was the out-front half of the partnership, came around five. She was the one in charge, Scott believed, both at work and at home. Missy Donaldson impressed him as a sweet little thing who looked at the world with a mixture of fear and wonder. More of the former than the latter, he guessed. Did McComb see herself as Missy's protector as well as her partner? Maybe. Probably.

He mounted the steps and rang the doorbell. At its chime, Dee and Dum began to bark in the backyard.

Deirdre opened the door. She was dressed in a pretty, figure-fitting dress that would no doubt look smashing as she stood at the hostess stand and then showed parties to their various tables. Her eyes were her best feature, a bewitching shade of greeny-gray and uptilted a bit at the corners.

'Oh, Mr Carey,' she said. 'How really nice to see you.' And the smile, which said how really *boring* to see

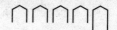

you. 'I'd love to invite you in, but I have to get down to the restaurant. Lots of reservations tonight. Leaf-peepers, you know.'

'I won't keep you,' Scott said, smiling his own smile. 'I just dropped by to show you this.' And he held up his iPad, so she could observe Dee and Dum squatting on his front lawn and shitting in tandem.

She looked at it for a long time, the smile fading. Seeing that didn't give him as much pleasure as he had expected.

'All right,' she said at last. The artificial lilt had gone out of her voice. Without it she sounded tired and older than her years, which might number thirty. 'You win.'

'It's not about winning, believe me.' As it came out of his mouth, Scott remembered a college teacher once remarking that when someone added *believe me* to a sentence, you should be aware.

'You've made your point, then. I can't come down and pick it up now, and Missy's already at work, but I will after we close. You won't even need to turn on your porch light. I should be able to see the . . . leavings . . . by the streetlight.'

'You don't need to do that.' Scott was starting to feel slightly mean. And in the wrong, somehow. *You win,* she'd said. 'I've already bagged it up. I just . . .'

23

'What? Wanted to get one up on me? If that was it, mission accomplished. From now on Missy and I will do our running down in the park. There will be no need for you to report us to the local authorities. Thank you, and good evening.' She started to close the door.

'Wait a second,' Scott said. 'Please.'

She looked at him through the half-closed door, face expressionless.

'Going to the animal control guy over a few piles of dog crap never crossed my mind, Ms McComb. Look, I just want us to be good neighbors. My only problem was the way you brushed me off. Refused to take me seriously. That isn't how good neighbors do. At least not around here.'

'Oh, we know exactly how good neighbors *do*,' she said. 'Around *here*.' The slightly superior smile came back, and she closed the door with it still on her face. Not before, however, he had seen a gleam in her eyes that might have been tears.

We know exactly how good neighbors do around here, he thought, walking back down the hill. What the hell did that mean?

Doctor Bob called him two days later, to ask if there had been any change. Scott told him things were

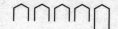

progressing as before. He was down to 207.6. 'It's pretty damn regular. Getting on the bathroom scale is like watching the numbers go backward on a car odometer.'

'But still no change in your physical dimensions? Waist size? Shirt size?'

'I'm still a forty waist and a thirty-four leg. I don't need to tighten my belt. Or let it out, although I'm eating like a lumberjack. Eggs, bacon, and sausage for breakfast. Sauces on everything at night. Got to be at least three thousand calories a day. Maybe four. Did you do any research?'

'I did,' Doctor Bob said. 'So far as I can tell, there's never been a case like yours. There are plenty of clinical reports about people whose metabolisms are in overdrive – people who eat, as you say, like lumberjacks and still stay thin – but no cases of people who weigh the same naked and dressed.'

'Oh, but it's so much more,' Scott said. He was smiling again. He smiled a lot these days, which was probably crazy, given the circumstances. He was losing weight like a late-stage cancer patient, but the work was going like gangbusters and he had never felt more cheerful. Sometimes, when he needed a break from the computer screen, he put on Motown and danced around the room with Bill D. Cat staring at him as if he'd gone mad.

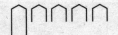

'Tell me the more.'

'This morning I weighed 208 flat. Straight out of the shower and buck naked. I got my hand-weights out of the closet, the twenty-pounders, and stepped on the scales with one in each hand. Still 208 flat.'

Silence on the other end for a moment, then Ellis said, 'You're shitting me.'

'Bob, if I'm lyin, I'm dyin.'

More silence. Then: 'It's as if you've got some kind of weight-repelling force-field around you. I know you don't want to be poked and prodded, but this is an entirely new thing. And it's big. There could be implications we can't even conceive of.'

'I don't want to be a freak,' Scott said. 'Put yourself in my place.'

'Will you at least think about it?'

'I have, a lot. And I have no urge to be a part of *Inside View*'s tabloid hall of fame, with my picture right between the Night Flier and Slender Man. Also, I've got my work to finish. I've promised Nora a share of the money even though the divorce was final before I got the job, and I'm pretty sure she can use it.'

'How long will that take?'

'Maybe six weeks. Of course there'll be revisions and test runs that will keep me busy into the new year, but six weeks to finish the main job.'

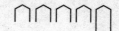

'If this continues at the same rate, you'd be down around 165 by then.'

'But still looking like a mighty man,' Scott said, and laughed. 'There's that.'

'You sound remarkably cheery, considering what's going on with you.'

'I *feel* cheerful. That might be nuts, but it's true. Sometimes I think this is the world's greatest weight-loss program.'

'Yes,' Ellis said, 'but where does it end?'

One day not long after his phone conversation with Doctor Bob, there came a light knock at Scott's front door. If he'd had his music turned up any louder – today it was the Ramones – he never would have heard it, and his visitor might have gone away. Probably with relief, because when he opened the front door, Missy Donaldson was standing there, and she looked scared half to death. It was the first time he'd seen her since taking the photos of Dee and Dum relieving themselves on his lawn. He supposed Deirdre had been as good as her word, and the women were now exercising their dogs in the town park. If they were allowing the boxers to run free down there, they really might run afoul of the animal control guy, no matter how well-behaved the dogs were. The park had a leash law. Scott had seen the signs.

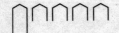

'Ms Donaldson,' he said. 'Hello.'

It was also the first time he'd seen her alone, and he was careful not to step over the threshold or make any sudden moves. She looked like she might leap down the steps and run away like a deer if he did. She was blond, not as pretty as her partner, but with a sweet face and clear blue eyes. There was a fragility about her, something that made Scott think of his mother's decorative china plates. It was hard to imagine this woman in a restaurant kitchen, moving from pot to pot and skillet to skillet through the steam, plating veggie dinners and bossing around the help while she did it.

'Can I help you? Would you like to come in? I have coffee . . . or tea, if you prefer.'

She was shaking her head before he was halfway through these standard offers of hospitality, and doing it hard enough to make her ponytail flip from one shoulder to the other. 'I just came to apologize. For Deirdre.'

'There's no need to do that,' he said. 'And no need to take your dogs all the way down to the park, either. All I ask is that you carry a couple of poop bags and check out my lawn on your way back. That's not too much to ask, is it?'

'No, not at all. I even suggested it to Deirdre. She almost snapped my head off.'

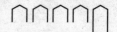

Scott sighed. 'I'm sorry to hear that. Ms Donaldson—'

'You can call me Missy, if you like.' Looking down and blushing slightly, as if she'd made a remark that might be taken for risqué.

'I would like that. Because all I want is for us to be good neighbors. Most of the folks up here on the View are, you know. And I seem to have gotten off on the wrong foot, although how I could have gotten off on the right one, I don't know.'

Still looking down, she said, 'We've been here for almost eight months, and the only time you've really talked to us – either of us – was when our dogs messed on your lawn.'

This was truer than Scott would have liked. 'I came up with a bag of doughnuts after you moved in,' he said (rather weakly), 'but you weren't at home.'

He thought she would ask why he hadn't tried again, but she didn't.

'I came to apologize for Deirdre, but I also wanted to explain her.' She raised her eyes to his. It took an obvious effort – her hands were clenched together at the waist of her jeans – but she did it. 'She's not mad at you, really . . . well, she is, but you're not the only one. She's mad at everybody. Castle Rock was a mistake. We came here because the place was almost business-ready, the price was right, and we wanted to get out

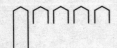

of the city – Boston, I mean. We knew it was a risk, but it seemed like an acceptable one. And the town is so beautiful. Well, you know that, I guess.'

Scott nodded.

'But we're probably going to lose the restaurant. If things don't turn around by Valentine's Day, for sure. That's the only reason she let them put her on that poster. She won't talk about how bad things are, but she knows it. We both do.'

'She said something about the leaf-peepers . . . and everyone says last summer was especially good . . .'

'The summer *was* good,' she said, speaking with a little more animation now. 'As for the leaf-peepers, we get some, but most of them go further west, into New Hampshire. North Conway has all those outlet stores to shop in, and more touristy stuff to do. I guess when winter comes we'll get the skiers passing through on their way to Bethel or Sugarloaf . . .'

Scott knew most skiers bypassed the Rock, taking Route 2 to the western Maine ski areas, but why bum her out more than she already was?

'Only when winter comes, we'd need the locals to pull us through. You know how it is, you must. The locals trade with other locals during the cold weather, and it's just enough to tide them over until the summer people come back. The hardware store, the lumberyard,

30

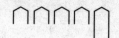

Patsy's Diner . . . they make do through the lean months. Only not many locals come to Frijole. Some, but not enough. Deirdre says it's not just because we're lesbians, but because we're *married* lesbians. I don't like to think she's right . . . but I think she is.'

'I'm sure . . .' He trailed off. That it isn't true? How in hell did he know, when he'd never even considered it?

'Sure of what?' she asked. Not in a snotty way, but in an honestly curious one.

He thought of his bathroom scale again, and the relentless way the numbers rolled back. 'Actually, I'm sure of nothing. If it's true, I'm sorry.'

'You should come down for dinner some night,' she said. This might have been a snide way of telling him she knew he'd never taken a meal at Holy Frijole, but he didn't think so. He didn't think this young woman had much in the way of snideness in her.

'I will,' he said. 'I assume you do have frijoles?'

She smiled. It lit her up. 'Oh yes, many kinds.'

He smiled back. 'Stupid question, I guess.'

'I have to go, Mr Carey—'

'Scott.'

She nodded. 'All right, Scott. It's good to talk to you. It took all my courage to come down here, but I'm glad I did.'

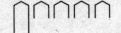

She held out her hand. Scott shook it.

'Just one favor. If you happen to see Deirdre, I'd appreciate you not mentioning that I came to see you.'

'Done deal,' Scott said.

The day after Missy Donaldson's visit, while he was sitting at the counter in Patsy's Diner and finishing his lunch, Scott heard someone behind him at one of the tables say something about 'that crack-snackin' restaurant.' Laughter followed. Scott looked at his half-eaten wedge of apple pie and the scoop of vanilla ice cream now puddling around it. It had looked good when Patsy set it down, but he no longer wanted it.

Had he heard such remarks before, and just filtered them out, the way he did with most overheard but unimportant (to him, at least) chatter? He didn't like to think so, but it was possible.

Probably going to lose the restaurant, she'd said. We'd have to count on the locals to pull us through.

She'd used the conditional tense, as if Holy Frijole already had a FOR SALE OR LEASE sign in the window.

He got up, left a tip under his dessert plate, and paid his check.

'Couldn't finish the pie?' Patsy asked.

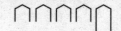

'My eyes were a little bigger than my stomach,' Scott said, which wasn't true. His eyes and stomach were the same size they'd always been; they just weighed less. The amazing thing was that he didn't care more, or even worry much. Unprecedented it might be, but sometimes his steady weight-loss slipped his mind completely. It had when he'd been waiting to snap photos of Dee and Dum squatting on his lawn. And it did now. What was on his mind at this moment was that crack about crack-snackers.

Four guys were sitting at the table the remark had come from, beefy fellows in work clothes. A row of hardhats sat in a line on the windowsill. The men were wearing orange vests with CRPW stenciled on them: Castle Rock Public Works.

Scott walked past them to the door, opened it, then changed his mind and went to the table where the road crew sat. He recognized two of the men, had played poker with one of them, Ronnie Briggs. Townies, like him. Neighbors.

'You know what, that was a shitty thing to say.'

Ronnie looked up, puzzled, then recognized Scott and grinned. 'Hey, Scotty, how you doin?'

Scott ignored him. 'Those women live just up the road from me. They're okay.' Well, Missy was. About McComb he wasn't so sure.

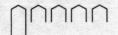

One of the other men crossed his arms over his broad chest and stared at Scott. 'Were you in this conversation?'

'No, but—'

'Right. So butt out.'

'—but I had to listen to it.'

Patsy's was small, but always crammed at lunchtime and filled with chatter. Now the talk and the busy gnash of forks on plates stopped. Heads turned. Patsy stood beside the cash register, alert for trouble.

'Once again, buddy, butt out. What we talk about is none of your business.'

Ronnie got up in a hurry. 'Hey, Scotty, why don't I walk out with you?'

'No need,' Scott said. 'I don't need an escort, but I have to say something first. If you eat there, the food is your business. You can criticize it all you want. What those women do in the rest of their lives is *not* your business. Got it?'

The one who had asked Scott if he had been invited into their conversation uncrossed his arms and stood up. He wasn't as tall as Scott, but he was younger and muscular. Red had crept up his broad neck and into his cheeks. 'You need to take your loud mouth out of here before I punch it for you.'

'None of that, none of that, now,' Patsy said sharply. 'Scotty, you need to leave.'

He stepped out of the diner without argument, and took a deep breath of the cool October air. There was a knock on the glass from behind him. Scott turned and saw Bull Neck looking out. He raised a finger as if to say *hang on a second*. There were all sorts of posters in Patsy's window. Bull Neck pulled one of them free, walked to the door, and opened it.

Scott balled his fists. He hadn't been in a fist-fight since grammar school (an epic battle that had lasted fifteen seconds, six punches thrown, four of them clean misses), but he was suddenly looking forward to this one. He felt light on his feet, more than ready. Not angry; happy. Optimistic.

Float like a butterfly, sting like a bee, he thought. Come on, big boy.

But Bull Neck didn't want to fight. He crumpled up the poster and threw it on the sidewalk at Scott's feet. 'Here's your girlfriend,' he said. 'Take it home and jerk off over it, why don't you? Short of rape, it's the closest you'll ever get to fucking her.'

He went back in and sat down with his mates, looking satisfied: case closed. Aware that everyone in the diner was looking at him through the window, Scott bent down, picked up the crumpled poster, and walked away toward noplace in particular, just wanting not to be stared at. He didn't feel ashamed of himself,

or stupid for starting something in the diner where half of the Rock ate lunch, but all those interested eyes were annoying. It made him wonder why anyone would want to get up on a stage to sing or act or tell jokes.

He smoothed out the ball of paper, and the first thing he thought of was something Missy Donaldson had said: *That's the only reason she let them put her on that poster.* 'Them,' it seemed, was the Castle Rock Turkey Trot Committee.

In the center of the sheet was a photo of Deirdre McComb. There were other runners, most of them behind her. A big number 19 was pinned to the waist-band of her tiny blue shorts. Above them was a tee-shirt with NEW YORK CITY MARATHON 2011 on the front. On her face was an expression Scott would not have associated with her: blissful happiness.

The caption read: *Deirdre McComb, co-owner of Holy Frijole, Castle Rock's newest fine dining experience, nears the finish line of the New York City Marathon, where she finished FOURTH in the Women's Division! She's announced that she will run in this year's Castle Rock 12K, the Turkey Trot. HOW ABOUT YOU?*

The details were below the caption. Castle Rock's annual Thanksgiving race would take place on the Friday following the holiday, starting at the Rec Department on Castle View and finishing downtown,

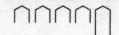

at the Tin Bridge. All ages were welcome, adult entrance fee five dollars for locals, seven dollars for out-of-towners, and two dollars for those under fifteen, sign up at the Castle Rock Rec Department.

Looking at the bliss on the face of the woman in the photo – runner's high at its purest – Scott understood that Missy hadn't been exaggerating about Holy Frijole's life-expectancy. Not in the slightest. Deirdre McComb was a proud woman with a high opinion of herself, and quick – much too quick, in Scott's opinion – to take offense. Her allowing her picture to be used this way, probably just for that mention of 'Castle Rock's newest fine dining experience,' had to be a Hail Mary pass. Anything, anything at all, to bring in a few more customers, if only to admire those long legs standing beside the hostess station.

He folded the poster, tucked it into the back pocket of his jeans, and walked slowly down Main Street, looking in shop windows as he went. There were posters in all of them – posters for bean suppers, posters for this year's giant yard sale in the parking lot of Oxford Plains Speedway, posters for Beano at the Catholic church and a potluck dinner at the fire station. He saw the Turkey Trot poster in the window of Castle Rock Computer Sales & Service, but nowhere else until he reached the Book Nook, a tiny building at the end of the street.

He went in, browsed a little, and grabbed a picture book from the discount table: *New England Fixtures and Furnishings*. Might not be anything in it he could use in his project – where the first stage was nearing completion, anyway – but you never knew. While he was paying Mike Badalamente, the owner and sole employee, he remarked on the poster in the window, and mentioned that the woman on it was his neighbor.

'Yeah, Deirdre McComb was a star runner for almost ten years,' Mike said, bagging up his book. 'She would have been in the Olympics back in '12, except she broke her ankle. Tough luck. Never even tried out in '16, I understand. I guess she's retired from the major competitions now, but I can't wait to run with her this year.' He grinned. 'Not that I'll be running with her long, once the starting gun goes off. She'll blow the competition away.'

'Men as well as women?'

Mike laughed. 'Buddy, they didn't call her the Malden Flash for nothing. Malden's where she originally came from.'

'I saw a poster in Patsy's, and one in the window of the computer store, and the one in your window. Nowhere else. What's up with that?'

Mike's smile went away. 'Nothing to be proud of. She's a lesbian. That would probably be okay if she

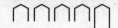

kept it to herself – no one cares what goes on behind closed doors – but she has to introduce that one who cooks at Frijole as her wife. Lot of people around here see that as a big old screw you.'

'So businesses won't put up the posters, even though the entry fees benefit the Rec? Just because she's on them?'

After having Bull Neck throw the poster from the diner at him, these weren't even real questions, just a way of getting it straight in his mind. In a way he felt as he had at ten, when the brother of his best friend had sat the younger boys down and told them the facts of life. Now as then, Scott had had a vague idea of the whole, but the specifics were still amazing to him. People really did that? Yes, they did. Apparently they did this, as well.

'They're going to be replaced with new ones,' Mike said. 'I happen to know, because I'm on the committee. It was Mayor Coughlin's idea. You know Dusty, the king of compromise. The new ones will show a bunch of turkeys running down Main Street. I don't like it, and I didn't vote for it, but I understand the rationale. The town just gives the Rec a pittance, two thousand dollars. That's not enough to maintain the playground, let alone all the other stuff we do. The Turkey Trot brings in almost *five* thousand, but we have to get the word out.'

'So . . . just because she's a lesbian . . .'

'A *married* lesbian. That's a deal-breaker for lots of folks. You know what Castle County's like, Scott, you've lived here for what, twenty-five years?'

'Over thirty.'

'Yeah, and solid Republican. *Conservative* Republican. The county went for Trump three-to-one in '16 and they think our stonebrain governor walks on water. If those women had kept it on the down-low they would have been fine, but they didn't. Now there are people who think they're trying to make some kind of statement. Myself, I think they were either ignorant about the political climate here or plain stupid.' He paused. 'Good food, though. Have you been there?'

'Not yet,' Scott said, 'but I plan to go.'

'Well, don't wait too long,' Mike said. 'Come next year at this time, there's apt to be an ice cream shop in there.'

CHAPTER 2

Holy Frijole

INSTEAD OF GOING HOME, as he had intended, Scott walked to the town common to page through his new purchase and look at the photos. He strolled along the other side of Main and saw what he now thought of as the Deirdre Poster one more time, in the knit and yarn shop. Nowhere else.

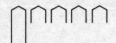

Mike had kept saying *they* and *those women*, but he really doubted that. It was all about McComb. She was the in-your-face half of the partnership. He thought Missy Donaldson would have been happy to keep it on the DL. That half of the partnership would have serious problems saying boo to a goose.

But *she came to see me,* he thought, *and she said a lot more than boo. That took guts.*

Yes, and he had liked her for it.

He put *New England Fixtures and Furnishings* on the park bench, and began to jog up and down the steps of the bandstand. It wasn't exercise he craved, just movement. *I've got ants in my pants,* he thought. *Not to mention bees in my knees.* And it wasn't like climbing the steps, more like springing up them. He did it half a dozen times, then went back to his bench, interested to find he wasn't out of breath, and his pulse was only slightly elevated.

He took out his phone and called Doctor Bob. The first thing Ellis asked about was his weight.

'204 as of this morning,' Scott said. 'Listen, have you—'

'So it's continuing. Have you thought any more about getting serious and really digging into this? Because a loss of forty pounds, give or take, *is* serious. I still have contacts at Mass General, and I don't think

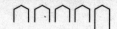

a total soup-to-nuts exam would cost you a dime. In fact, they might pay you.'

'Bob, I feel fine. Better than fine, actually. The reason I called was to ask if you've eaten at Holy Frijole yet.'

There was a pause while Ellis digested this change of subject. Then he said, 'The one your lesbian neighbors run? No, not yet.'

Scott frowned. 'You know what, there might be a little more to them than their sexual orientation. Just sayin'.'

'Mellow out.' Ellis sounded slightly taken aback. 'I didn't mean to step on your corns.'

'Okay. It's just . . . there was an incident at lunch. At Patsy's.'

'What kind of incident?'

'A little argument. Over them. Doesn't matter. Listen, Bob, how about a night out? Holy Frijole. Dinner. I'll buy.'

'When were you thinking?'

'How about tonight?'

'I can't tonight, but I could on Friday. Myra's going to spend the weekend at her sister's down in Manchester, and I'm a lousy cook.'

'It's a date,' Scott said.

'A man-date,' Ellis agreed. 'Next you'll be asking me to marry you.'

'That would be bigamy on your part,' Scott said, 'and I will lead you not into temptation. Just do one thing for me – you make the reservation.'

'Still sideways with them?' Ellis sounded amused. 'Wouldn't it be better to just give it a pass? There's a nice Italian place in Bridgton.'

'Nope. I've got my face fixed for Mexican.'

Doctor Bob sighed. 'I guess I can make the reservation, although if what I'm hearing about that place is true, I hardly think one will be necessary.'

Scott picked Ellis up on Friday, because Doctor Bob no longer liked to drive at night. The ride down to the restaurant was short, but long enough for Bob to tell Scott the real reason he had wanted to put off their man-date until Friday: he didn't want to get into a squabble with Myra, who was on church and town committees that had no love for the two women who ran the Rock's newest fine dining experience.

'You're kidding,' Scott said.

'Unfortunately not. Myra's open-minded on most subjects, but when it comes to sexual politics . . . let's just say she was raised a certain way. We might have argued, perhaps even bitterly, if I didn't believe shouting matches between husband and wife in old age are undignified.'

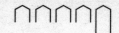

'Will you tell her you visited the Rock's Mexican-vegetarian den of iniquity?'

'If she asks where I ate on Friday night, yes. Otherwise I'll keep my mouth shut. As will you.'

'As will I,' Scott said. He pulled into one of the slant parking spaces. 'Here we are. Thanks for doing this with me, Bob. I'm hoping it will put things right.'

It did not.

Deirdre was at the hostess stand, not wearing a dress tonight but a white shirt and tapered black slacks that showcased those admirable legs. Doctor Bob entered ahead of Scott, and she smiled at him – not the slightly superior one, with the lips closed and the eyebrows raised, but a professionally welcoming one. Then she saw Scott, and the smile went away. She gave him a cool appraisal with those green-gray eyes, as if he were a bug on a microscope slide, then dropped them and grabbed a couple of menus.

'Let me show you to your table.'

As she led them to it, Scott admired the decor. It wasn't enough to say McComb and Donaldson had taken pains; this looked like a labor of love. Mexican music – he thought the type they called Tejano or ranchera – played from the overhead speakers. The walls were soft yellow, and the plaster had been roughed up

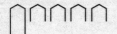

to look like adobe. The sconces were green glass cacti. Large wall hangings featured a sun, a moon, two dancing monkeys, and a frog with golden eyes. The room was twice the size of Patsy's Diner, but he saw only five couples and a single party of four.

'Here you are,' Deirdre said. 'I hope you enjoy your meal.'

'I'm sure we will,' Scott said. 'It's good to be here. I'm sort of hoping we can start over, Ms McComb. Do you think that would be possible?'

She looked at him calmly, but without warmth. 'Gina will be right with you, and she'll tell you the specials.'

With that she was gone.

Doctor Bob seated himself and shook out his napkin. 'Warm packs, gently applied to the cheeks and brow.'

'Beg your pardon?'

'Treatment for frostbite. I believe you just took a cold blast, directly to the face.'

Before Scott could reply, a waitress appeared – the only waitress, it seemed. Like Deirdre McComb, she was dressed in black pants and a white shirt. 'Welcome to Holy Frijole. Could I bring you gentlemen anything to drink?'

Scott asked for a Coke. Ellis opted for a glass of the house wine, then put on his specs for a better look at the young woman. 'You're Gina Ruckleshouse, aren't

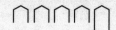

you? You must be. Your mother was my PA when I still had my office downtown, back in the Jurassic Era. You bear a strong resemblance to her.'

She smiled. 'I'm Gina Beckett now, but that's right.'

'Very good to see you, Gina. Give my regards to your mom.'

'I will. She's at Dartmouth-Hitchcock now, over on the dark side.' Meaning New Hampshire. 'I'll be right back to tell you about the specials.'

When she returned, she brought appetizers with their drinks, setting the plates down almost reverently. The smell was to die for.

'What have we got here?' Scott asked.

'Freshly fried green plantain chips, and a salsa of garlic, cilantro, lime, and a little green chile. Compliments of the chef. She says it's more Cuban than Mexican, but she hopes that won't keep you from enjoying it.'

When Gina left, Doctor Bob leaned forward, smiling. 'Seems you've had some success with the one in the kitchen, at least.'

'Maybe you're the favored one. Gina could have whispered in Missy's ear that her mother used to labor in your medical sweatshop.' Although Scott knew better . . . or thought he did.

Doctor Bob waggled his shaggy white eyebrows. 'Missy, eh? On a first-name basis with her, are we?'

'Come on, Doc, quit it.'

'I will, if you promise not to call me Doc. I hate it. Makes me think of Milburn Stone.'

'Who's that?'

'Google it when you get home, my child.'

They ate, and they ate well. The food was meatless but terrific: enchiladas with frijoles and tortillas that had obviously not come from a supermarket package. As they ate, Scott told Ellis about his little set-to in Patsy's, and about the posters featuring Deirdre McComb, soon to be replaced by less controversial ones starring a flock of cartoon turkeys. He asked if Myra had been on that committee.

'No, that's one she missed . . . but I'm sure she would have approved the change.'

With that he turned the conversation back to Scott's mysterious weight-loss, and the more mysterious fact that he appeared not to have changed physically. And, of course, the most mysterious fact of all: whatever he wore or carried that was supposed to weigh him down . . . didn't.

A few more people came in, and the reason McComb was dressed like a waitress became clear: she *was* one, at least tonight. Maybe every night. The fact that she was doing double duty made the restaurant's economic position even clearer. The corner-cutting had begun.

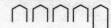

Gina asked them if they wanted dessert. Both demurred. 'I couldn't eat another bite, but please tell Ms Donaldson it was superb,' Scott said.

Doctor Bob put two thumbs up.

'She'll be so pleased,' Gina said. 'I'll be back with your check.'

The restaurant was emptying rapidly, only a few couples left, sipping after-dinner drinks. Deirdre was asking those departing how their meals had been, and thanking them for coming. Big smiles. But no smiles for the two men at the table beneath the frog tapestry; not even a single look in their direction.

It's as if we have the plague, Scott thought.

'And you're sure you feel fine?' Doctor Bob asked, for perhaps the tenth time. 'No heartbeat arrhythmia? No dizzy spells? Excessive thirst?'

'None of that. Pretty much the opposite. Want to hear an interesting thing?'

He told Ellis about jogging up and down the bandstand steps – almost *bouncing* up and down them – and how he had taken his pulse afterward. 'Not resting pulse, but pretty damn low. Under eighty. Also, I'm not a doctor, but I know what my body looks like, and there's been no wasting in the muscles.'

'Not yet, anyway,' Ellis said.

'I don't think there's going to be. I think mass stays

the same, even though the weight that should go with mass is somehow disappearing.'

'The idea is insane, Scott.'

'Couldn't agree more, but there it is. The power gravity has over me has definitely been lessened. And who couldn't be cheerful about that?'

Before Doctor Bob could reply, Gina came back with the slip for Scott to sign. He did so, adding a generous tip, and told her again how good everything had been.

'That's wonderful. Please come again. And tell your friends.' She bent forward and lowered her voice. 'We *really* need the business.'

Deirdre McComb wasn't at the hostess stand when they went out; she was standing on the sidewalk at the foot of the steps and gazing toward the stoplight at the Tin Bridge. She turned to Ellis and gave him a smile. 'I wonder if I could have a word with Mr Carey in private? It won't take a minute.'

'Of course. Scott, I'm going across the street to inspect the contents of the bookshop window. Just give me a honk when you're ready to roll.'

Doctor Bob crossed Main Street (deserted as it usually was by eight o'clock; the town tucked in early) and Scott turned to Deirdre. Her smile was gone. He

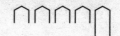

saw she was angry. He had hoped to make things better by eating at Holy Frijole, but instead he had made them worse. He didn't know why that should be, but it pretty clearly was.

'What's on your mind, Ms McComb? If it's still the dogs—'

'How could it be, when we now run them in the park? Or try to, at least. Their leashes are always getting tangled.'

'You can run them on the View,' he said. 'I told you that. It's just a matter of picking up their—'

'Never mind the dogs.' Those green-gray eyes were all but snapping off sparks. 'That subject is closed. What *needs* to be closed is your behavior. We don't need you standing up for us in the local grease-pit, and restarting a lot of talk that had just begun to die down.'

If you believe it's dying down, you haven't seen how few shop windows have your picture in them, Scott thought. What he said was, 'Patsy's is the farthest thing in the world from a grease-pit. She may not serve your kind of food there, but it's clean.'

'Clean or dirty, that's not the point. If standing up needs to be done, *I'll* do it. I – we – don't need you to play Sir Galahad. For one thing, you're a little too old for the part.' Her eyes flicked down his shirt front. 'For another, you're a little too overweight.'

Given Scott's current condition, this jab entirely missed the mark, but he felt a certain sour amusement at her employment of it; she would have been infuriated to hear a man say some woman was a little too old and a little too overweight to play the part of Guinevere.

'I hear you,' he said. 'Point taken.'

She seemed momentarily disconcerted by the mildness of his reply – as if she had swung at an easy target and somehow missed entirely.

'Are we done, Ms McComb?'

'One other thing. I want you to stay away from my wife.'

So she knew he and Donaldson had talked, and now it was Scott's turn to hesitate. Had Missy told McComb that she had gone to Scott, or had she, perhaps in order to keep the peace, told McComb that Scott had come to her? If he asked, he might get her in trouble, and he didn't want to do that. He was no marriage expert – his own being a fine case in point – but he thought the problems with the restaurant were already putting the couple's relationship under enough strain.

'All right,' he said. '*Now* are we done?'

'Yes.' And, as she had at the end of their first meeting, before closing the door in his face: 'Good discussion.'

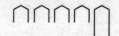

He watched her mount the steps, slim and quick in her black pants and white shirt. He could see her running up and down the bandstand steps, much faster than he could manage even after dropping forty pounds, and as light on her feet as a ballerina. What was it Mike Badalamente had said? *I can't wait to run with her, not that I'll be running with her long.*

God had given her a beautiful body for running, and Scott wished to God she was enjoying it more. He guessed that, behind the superior smile, Deirdre McComb wasn't enjoying much these days.

'Ms McComb?'

She turned. Waited.

'It really was a fine meal.'

No smile for this, superior or otherwise. 'Good. I suppose you've already passed that on to Missy by way of Gina, but I'm happy to pass it on again. And now that you've been here, and shown yourself to be on the side of the politically correct angels, why don't you stick to Patsy's? I think we'll all be more comfortable that way.'

She went inside. Scott stood on the sidewalk for a moment, feeling . . . what? It was such a weird mix of emotions that he guessed there was no single word for it. Chastened, yes. Slightly amused, check. A bit pissed off. But most of all, sad. Here was a woman who didn't want an olive branch, and he had believed – naively, it seemed – that everyone wanted one of those.

Probably Doctor Bob's right and I'm still a child, he thought. Hell, I don't even know who Milburn Stone was.

The street was too quiet for him to feel okay about even a short honk, so he went across the street and stood beside Ellis at the window of the Book Nook.

'Get it straightened out?' Doctor Bob asked.

'Not exactly. She told me to leave her wife alone.'

Doctor Bob turned to him. 'Then I suggest you do that.'

He drove Ellis home, and mercifully, Doctor Bob didn't spend any of the trip importuning Scott to check into Mass General, the Mayo, the Cleveland Clinic, or NASA. Instead, as he got out, he thanked Scott for an interesting evening and told him to stay in touch.

'Of course I will,' Scott said. 'We're sort of in this together now.'

'That being the case, I wonder if you'd come over, perhaps Sunday. Myra won't be back and we could watch the Patriots upstairs instead of in my poor excuse for a man-cave. Also, I'd like to take some measurements. Start keeping a record. Would you allow that much?'

'Yes to the football, no to the measurements,' Scott said. 'At least for now. Okay?'

ELEVATION

'I accept your decision,' Doctor Bob said. 'That really was a fine meal. I didn't miss the meat at all.'

'Neither did I,' Scott said, but this wasn't precisely true. When he got home, he made himself a salami sandwich with brown mustard. Then he stripped and stepped on the bathroom scale. He had declined the measurements because he was sure Doctor Bob would also want a weigh-in each time he checked Scott's muscle density, and he had an intuition – or perhaps it was some deep physical self-knowledge – which now proved to be correct. He had been at a little over 201 that morning. Now, after a big dinner followed by a hefty snack, he was at 199.

The process was speeding up.

CHAPTER 3

The Wager

THAT WAS A GORGEOUS late October in Castle Rock, with day after day of cloudless blue skies and warm temperatures. The politically progressive minority spoke of global warming; the more conservative majority called it an especially fine Indian summer

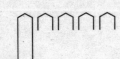

that would soon be followed by a typical Maine winter; everyone enjoyed it. Pumpkins came out on stoops, black cats and skeletons danced in the windows of houses, trick-or-treaters were duly warned at an elementary school assembly to stay on the sidewalks when the big night came, and only take wrapped treats. The high schoolers went in costume to the annual Halloween dance in the gym, for which a local garage band, Big Top, renamed themselves Pennywise and the Clowns.

In the two weeks or so since his dinner with Ellis, Scott continued to lose weight at a slowly accelerating pace. He was down to 180, a total drop of sixty pounds, but he continued to feel fine, tip-top, in the pink. On Halloween afternoon he drove to the CVS drugstore in Castle Rock's new strip mall, and bought more Halloween candy than he would probably need. Residents of the View didn't get a lot of costumed customers these days (there had been more before the collapse of the Suicide Stairs a few years earlier), but whatever the little beggars didn't take, he would eat himself. One of the benefits of his peculiar condition, aside from all the extra energy, was how he could eat as much as he wanted without turning into a podge. He supposed all the fats might be playing hell with his cholesterol, but he had an idea they

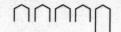

weren't. He was in the best shape of his life, despite the deceptive roll hanging over his belt, and his frame of mind was better than it had been since the days when his courtship of Nora Kenner had been in full flower.

In addition to all that, his department store clients were delighted with his work, convinced (fallaciously, Scott was afraid) that the multiple websites he had crafted would turn their bricks-and-mortar business around. He had recently received a check for $582,674.50. Before banking it, he photographed it. He was sitting here in a little Maine town, working from his home study, and he was next door to rich.

He had seen Deirdre and Missy only twice, and from a distance. Running in the park, Dee and Dum on long leashes and not looking happy about it.

When Scott got back from his drugstore errand, he started up his walk, then diverted to the elm tree in his front yard. The leaves had turned, but thanks to the warmth of that fall season, most of them were still on the tree, rustling gently. The lowest branch was six feet over his head, and it looked inviting. He dropped the bag with the candy in it, raised his arms, flexed his knees, and jumped. He caught the branch easily, a thing he couldn't have come close to doing a year ago. No wasting in his muscles; they still thought they were supporting a man who weighed 240. It made him think of old TV footage, showing the astronauts who'd landed on the moon taking ginormous leaps.

He dropped to the lawn, picked up the bag, and went to the porch steps. Instead of walking up them, he flexed again and jumped all the way to the stoop.

It was easy.

He put the candy in a bowl by the front door, and went into his study. He turned on his computer, but didn't open any of the work-files scattered across the desktop. He opened the calendar function instead, and called up the following year. The date numbers were in black, except for holidays and appointments. Those were in red. Scott had marked only one appointment for next year: May 3rd. The notation, also in red, consisted of a single word: ZERO. When he deleted it, May 3rd turned black again. He selected March 31st, and typed ZERO in the square. That now looked to him like the day when he would run out of weight, unless the rate of loss kept speeding up. Which might happen. In the meantime, however, he intended to enjoy life. Scott felt he owed it to himself. After all, how many people with a terminal condition could say they felt absolutely fine? Sometimes he thought of a saying Nora had brought

home from her AA meetings: *the past is history, the future's a mystery.*

It seemed to fit his current situation pretty well.

He got his first costumed customers around four o'clock, and the last ones just past sunset. There were ghosts and goblins, superheroes and stormtroopers. One child was amusingly got up as a blue and white post office box, with his eyes peeking out through the slot. Scott gave most of the kids two of the mini-sized candybars, but the mailbox got three, because he was the best. The younger children were accompanied by their parents. The latecomers, a bit older, were mostly on their own.

The last pair, a boy-girl combo who were supposed to be – maybe – Hansel and Gretel, showed up at just after six thirty. Scott gave them each a couple of treats so they wouldn't trick him (around nine or ten, they didn't look particularly tricksy), and asked if they'd seen any others in the neighborhood.

'Nope,' the boy said, 'I think we're the last ones.' He elbowed the girl. '*She* kept wanting to fix her hair.'

'What did you get up the street?' Scott asked, pointing to the house where McComb and Donaldson lived. 'Anything nice?' It had just occurred to him that Missy might have created some special Halloween treats,

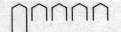

chocolate-dipped carrot sticks, or something of that ilk.

The little girl's eyes went round. 'Our mother told us not to go there, because those aren't nice ladies.'

'They're lesbeans,' the boy amplified. 'Daddy said so.'

'Ah,' Scott said. 'Lesbeans. I see. You kids get home safe, now. Stay on the sidewalks.'

They went on their way, toting their sacks of sugary treats. Scott closed his door and looked into the candy bowl. It was still half full. He thought he'd gotten sixteen or maybe eighteen customers. He wondered how many McComb and Donaldson had gotten. He wondered if they had gotten any.

He went into the living room, turned on the news, saw video of kids trick-or-treating in Portland, and then turned it off again.

Not-nice ladies, he thought. Lesbeans. Daddy said so.

An idea came to him then, the way his coolest ideas sometimes did: almost completely formed, needing nothing but a few tweaks and a little polish. Cool ideas weren't necessarily *good* ideas, of course, but he intended to follow up on this one and find out.

'Treat yourself,' he said, and laughed. 'Treat yourself before you dry up and disappear. Why not? Just why the fuck not?'

★

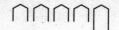

Scott walked into the Castle Rock Rec at nine the next morning with a five-dollar bill in his hand. Sitting at the Turkey Trot 12K sign-up table were Mike Badalamente and Ronnie Briggs, the Public Works guy Scott had last seen in Patsy's. Behind them, in the gymnasium, a morning league was playing pick-up basketball, shirts versus skins.

'Hey, Scotty!' Ronnie said. 'How're you doing, m'man?'

'Fine,' Scott said. 'You?'

'Pert!' Ronnie exclaimed. 'Just as pert as ever I could be, although they cut my hours at the PW. Haven't seen you at Thursday night poker lately.'

'Been working pretty hard, Ronnie. Big project.'

'Well, you know what, about that thing in Patsy's . . .' Ronnie looked embarrassed. 'Man, I'm sorry about that. Trevor Yount, he's got a big mouth, and nobody likes to shut him up when he goes on one of his rants. Apt to get a bust nose for your trouble if you try it.'

'That's all right, water under the bridge. Hey, Mike, can I sign up for the race?'

'You bet,' Mike said. 'The more the merrier. You can keep me company at the back of the pack, along with the kids, the old, and the out of shape. We've even got a blind guy this year. Going to run with his service dog, he says.'

Ronnie leaned over the table and patted Scott's front porch. 'And don't worry about this, Scotty my boy, they've got EMTs at each 3K mark, and two at the finish line. If you vapor lock, they'll kick-start you.'

'Good to know.'

Scott paid his five dollars and signed a waiver stating the town of Castle Rock would not be held responsible for any accidents or medical problems he might incur during the seven-and-a-half-mile race. Ronnie scrawled a receipt; Mike gave him a map of the racecourse and a number placard. 'Just pull off the backing and stick it to your shirt before the race. Give your name to one of the starters so they can check you off and you're good to go.'

The number he'd been assigned, Scott saw, was 371, and this was still over three weeks before the big race. He whistled. 'You're off to a good start, especially if these are all adult entry fees.'

'They're not,' Mike said, 'but most are, and if this is like last year, we'll end up having eight or nine hundred running. They come from all over New England. God knows why, but our piddling little Turkey Trot has somehow become a big deal. My kids would say it's gone viral.'

'Scenery,' Ronnie said. 'That's what brings em. Plus the hills, especially Hunter's. And accourse the winner gets to light the Christmas tree in the town square.'

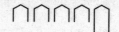

'The Rec has all the concessions along the route,' Mike said. 'As far as I'm concerned, that's the beauty part. We're talking a lot of hotdogs, popcorn, soda, and hot chocolate.'

'No beer, though,' Ronnie said sadly. 'They voted it down again this year. Just like the casino.'

And the lesbeans, Scott thought. The town voted down the lesbeans, too. Just not at the ballot box. The town motto seems to be if you can't keep it on the down-low, then out you must go.

'Is Deirdre McComb still planning to run?' Scott asked.

'Oh, you bet,' Mike said. 'And she's got her old number. 19. We saved it for her special.'

Scott took Thanksgiving dinner with Bob and Myra Ellis, plus two of their five grown children – the ones who lived within driving distance. Scott had two helpings of everything, then joined the kids in a spirited game of tag in the Ellises' large backyard.

'He'll have a heart attack, running around after all that food,' Myra said.

'I don't think so,' Doctor Bob said. 'He's prepping for the big race tomorrow.'

'If he tries anything more than just jogging in that 12K, he *will* have a heart attack,' Myra said, watching

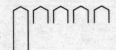

Scott chase down one of her laughing grandchildren. 'I swan, men in middle age lose all their sense.'

Scott went home tired and happy and looking forward to the Turkey Trot the next day. Before bed, he got on the scale and observed without much surprise that he was down to 141. He wasn't losing two pounds a day yet, not quite, but that would come. He turned on his computer and slid Zero Day back to March 15th. He was afraid – it would have been foolish not to be – but he was also curious. And something else. Happy? Was that it? Yes. Probably crazy, but definitely yes. Certainly he felt singled out somehow. Doctor Bob might think *that* was crazy, but Scott thought it was sane. Why feel bad about what you couldn't change? Why not embrace it?

There had been a cold snap in the middle of November, one hard enough to frost the fields and lawns, but the Friday after Thanksgiving dawned overcast and warm for the season. Charlie Lopresti on channel 13 was forecasting rain for later, perhaps heavy, but it hadn't put a dent in Castle Rock's big day, either among the spectators or the contestants.

Scott put on his old running shorts and walked up to the Rec building at quarter of eight, over an hour before the Trot was scheduled to commence, and there

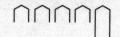

was already a huge crowd there, most of them wearing zip-up hoodies (which would be discarded at various points along the route as bodies warmed). The majority were waiting to check in on the left, where signs read OUT OF TOWN RUNNERS. On the right, where the sign read CASTLE ROCK RESIDENTS, there was a short single file. Scott pulled the backing from his number and pasted it on his tee-shirt, above the bulge of his bogus belly. Nearby, the high school band was tuning up.

Patsy Denton, of Patsy's Diner, checked him in and directed him toward the far side of the building, where View Drive started and the race would begin.

'Being local, you could cheat up to the front,' Patsy said, 'but it's generally considered bad form. You should find the other three hundreds, and stick with them.' She eyed his midsection. 'Besides, you'll be runnin at the back with the kiddies soon enough.'

'Ouch,' Scott said.

She smiled. 'Truth hurts, doesn't it? All those bacon-burgers and cheese omelets have a way of comin back to haunt a fella. Bear it in mind if you start to feel your chest tightenin up.'

As Scott walked over to join the growing crowd of the locals who had checked in early, he studied the little map. The course was a rough loop. Down View

67

Drive to Route 117 was the first three kilometers. The Bowie Stream covered bridge was the halfway point. Then along Route 119, which became Bannerman Road once it crossed the municipal town line. The tenth kilometer included Hunter's Hill, sometimes known as Runners' Heartbreak. It was so steep the kids often went tobogganing there on snowdays, picking up fearsome speed but kept safe by the plowed banks. The last two kilometers were along Castle Rock's Main Street, which would be lined with cheering spectators, not to mention camera crews from all three of the Portland TV stations.

Everyone was milling in groups, talking and laughing, drinking hot coffee or cocoa. Everyone, that was, except for Deirdre McComb, looking impossibly tall and beautiful in her blue shorts and a pair of snow-white Adidas sneaks. She had placed her number – 19 – off-center, high on the left side of her bright red tee-shirt, in order to leave most of the shirt's front visible. On it was an empanada and HOLY FRIJOLE 142 MAIN STREET.

Advertising the restaurant made sense . . . but only if she thought it would do any good. Scott had an idea she might be beyond that now. Surely she knew that 'her' posters had been replaced by less controversial ones; unlike the fellow who would be running with

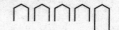

his guide dog (Scott saw him near the starting line, giving an interview), she wasn't blind. That she hadn't just said fuck it and dropped out didn't surprise him; he had a pretty good idea of why she was hanging in there. She wanted to stick it to them.

Of course she does, he thought. She wants to beat them all – the men, the women, the kids, and the blind man with his German Shepherd. She wants the whole town to watch a lesbean, and a *married* lesbean at that, throw the switch on their Christmas tree.

He thought she knew the restaurant was toast, and maybe she was glad, maybe she couldn't wait to get the hell out of the Rock, but yes, she wanted to stick it to them before she and her wife went, and leave them with that memory. She wouldn't even have to make a speech, just smile that superior smile. The one that said *in your eye, you provincial, self-righteous assholes. Good discussion.*

She was limbering up, first lifting one leg behind her and holding it by the ankle, then the other. Scott stopped at the refreshment table (FREE TO RACERS, ONE TO A CUSTOMER) and got two coffees, paying a buck for the extra one. Then he walked over to Deirdre McComb. He had no designs on her, nor romantic inclinations of any kind, but he was a man, and could not help admiring her figure as she stretched and turned,

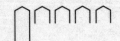

all the time looking raptly up at the sky, where there was nothing to be seen but slate-gray clouds.

Centering herself, he thought. Getting ready. Maybe not for her last race, but maybe for the last one that really means something to her.

'Hello,' he said. 'It's me again. The pest.'

She dropped her leg and looked at him. The smile appeared, as predictable as sunrise in the east. It was her armor. There might be someone behind it who was hurt as well as angry, but she had determined no one in the world would see that. Except, perhaps, for Missy. Who was not in evidence this morning.

'Why, it's Mr Carey,' she said. 'And sporting a number. Also a front porch, and I do believe it's a little bigger.'

'Flattery will get you nowhere,' he said. 'And hey, maybe it's just a pillow under there, something I wear to fool people.' He held out one of the cups. 'Would you like a coffee?'

'No. I had oatmeal and half a grapefruit at six this morning. That's all I'll take until halfway. Then I'll stop at one of the stands and help myself to a cranberry juice. Now, if you'll pardon me, I'd like to finish my stretches and my meditation.'

'Give me a minute,' Scott said. 'I didn't really come over to offer you a coffee, because I knew you wouldn't take it. I came to offer you a wager.'

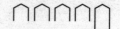

She had grasped her right ankle in her left hand and was starting to lift it behind her. Now she dropped it and stared at him as if he had grown a horn in the center of his forehead. 'What in God's name are you talking about? And how many times do I have to tell you that I find your efforts to . . . I don't know . . . *ingratiate* yourself to me are unwelcome?'

'There's a big difference between ingratiation and trying to be friendly, as I think you know. Or would, if you weren't always in such a defensive crouch.'

'I'm *not*—'

'But I'm sure you've got your reasons to feel defensive, and let's not argue semantics. The wager I'm offering is simple. If you win today, I'll never bother you again, and that includes complaining about your dogs. Run them on View Drive all you want, and if they poop on my lawn, *I'll* pick it up, with never a single word of protest.'

She looked incredulous. '*If* I win? *If*?'

He ignored this. 'If, on the other hand, I win today, you and Missy have to come to my house for dinner. A *vegetarian* dinner. I'm not a bad cook when I put my mind to it. We'll sit down, we'll drink a little wine, and we'll talk. Kind of break the ice, or at least try to. We don't have to be bosom buddies, I don't expect that, it's very hard to change a closed mind—'

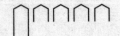

'My mind is *not* closed!'

'But maybe we can be real neighbors. I could borrow a cup of sugar from you, you could borrow a stick of butter from me, that kind of thing. If neither of us win, it's a push. Things can go on the way they have.'

Until your restaurant closes its doors and you two blow town, he thought.

'Let me make sure I'm hearing this. You're betting you can beat me today? Let me be frank, Mr Carey. Your body tells me that you're a typical over-indulgent, under-exercised white American male. If you push it, you'll either go down with leg cramps, a sprained back, or a heart attack. You will not beat me today. *Nobody* is going to beat me today. Now please go away and let me finish getting ready.'

'Okay,' Scott said, 'I get it. You're afraid to take the wager. I thought you might be.'

She was lifting her other leg now, but she dropped it. 'Jesus shined-up Christ on a trailer hitch. *Fine*. It's a bet. Now leave me alone.'

Smiling, Scott put out his hand. 'We have to shake on it. That way, if you back out, I can call you a welsher right to your face, and you'll have to suck it up.'

She snorted, but gave his hand a single hard grip. And for a moment – just one small glimmer of a moment – he saw a hint of a real smile. Only a trace,

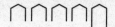

but he had an idea she had a fine one when she really let it rip.

'Great,' he said, then added, 'Good discussion.' He started away, back to the 300s.

'Mr Carey.'

He turned back.

'Why is this so important to you? Is it because I – because *we* – are a threat to your masculinity somehow?'

No, it's because I'm going to die next year, he thought, and I'd like to put at least one thing right before I do. It's not going to be my marriage, that's kaput, and it's not going to be the department store websites, because those guys don't understand that their stores are like buggy-whip factories at the start of the automobile age.

But those things he wouldn't say. She wouldn't understand. How could she, when he didn't fully understand himself?

'It just is,' he said finally.

He left her with that.

CHAPTER 4

The Turkey Trot

AT TEN MINUTES PAST nine, only a little late, Mayor
Dusty Coughlin stepped in front of over eight hundred
runners stretching back nearly a quarter of a mile. He
held a starter pistol in one hand and a battery-powered
bullhorn in the other. The low numbers, including

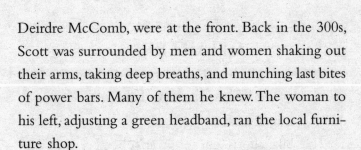

Deirdre McComb, were at the front. Back in the 300s, Scott was surrounded by men and women shaking out their arms, taking deep breaths, and munching last bites of power bars. Many of them he knew. The woman to his left, adjusting a green headband, ran the local furniture shop.

'Good luck, Milly,' he said.

She grinned and gave him a thumbs-up. 'Same to you.'

Coughlin raised the bullhorn. '*WELCOME TO THE FORTY-FIFTH ANNUAL TURKEY TROT! ARE YOU FOLKS READY?*'

The runners gave a yell of assent. One of the high school band members blew a flourish on his trumpet.

'*ALL RIGHT, THEN! ON YOUR MARK . . . GET SET . . .*'

The mayor, wearing his big politician's grin, raised the starter pistol and pulled the trigger. The bang seemed to echo off the low-hanging clouds.

'*GO!*'

The ones at the front moved forward smoothly. Deirdre was easy to spot in her bright red shirt. The rest of the runners were packed tightly together, and their start was not so smooth. A couple fell down and had to be helped up. Milly Jacobs was jostled forward into a pair of young men wearing biking shorts and

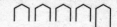

turned-around hats. Scott grabbed her arm and steadied her.

'Thanks,' she said. 'This is my fourth time, and it's always like this at the start. Like when they open the doors at a rock concert.'

The bike-shorts guys saw an opening, shot past Mike Badalamente and a trio of ladies who were talking and laughing as they jogged, and were gone, running in tandem.

Scott drew even with Mike and gave him a wave. Mike skimmed him a salute, then patted the left side of his chest and crossed himself.

Everyone believes I'm going to have a heart attack, Scott thought. You'd think whatever antic providence decided it would be interesting to make me lose weight could have at least buffed me out a little, but no.

Milly Jacobs – from whom Nora had once bought a dining room set – gave him a sideways grin. 'This is fun for the first half hour or so. Then it's heck. By the 8K mark it's hell. If you make it through that part, you catch a little following wind. Sometimes.'

'Sometimes, huh?' Scott said.

'Right. I'm hoping for that this year. I'd like to make it all the way. I've only managed that once. Good seeing you, Scott.' With that she picked up the pace and pulled ahead of him.

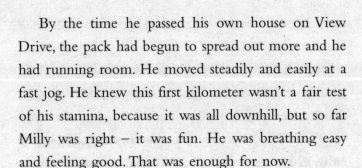

By the time he passed his own house on View Drive, the pack had begun to spread out more and he had running room. He moved steadily and easily at a fast jog. He knew this first kilometer wasn't a fair test of his stamina, because it was all downhill, but so far Milly was right – it was fun. He was breathing easy and feeling good. That was enough for now.

He passed a few runners, but only a few. More passed him, some from the 500s, some from the 600s, and one speed-devil with 721 pasted to his shirt. This comical fellow had a spinning whirligig mounted on his hat. Scott was in no particular hurry, at least not yet. He could see Deirdre on every straight stretch, maybe four hundred yards ahead. Her red shirt and blue shorts were impossible to miss. She was taking it easy. There were at least a dozen runners ahead of her, maybe even two dozen, and that didn't surprise Scott. This wasn't her first rodeo, and unlike most of the amateurs, she would have a carefully thought-out plan. Scott guessed she would allow others to set the pace until the eighth or ninth K, then start pulling ahead of them one by one and not take the lead until Hunter's Hill. She might even make it exciting by waiting until downtown to put on her final burst, but he didn't think so. She would want to win going away.

He felt the lightness in his feet, the strength in his

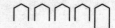

legs, and resisted the urge to speed up. Just keep the red shirt in your sights, he told himself. She knows what she's doing, so let her guide you.

At the intersection of View Drive and Route 117, Scott passed a little orange marker: 3K. Ahead of him were the bike-shorts guys, one pounding along on either side of the yellow centerline. They passed a couple of teenagers, and Scott did likewise. The teenagers looked to be in good shape, but they were already breathing hard. As he left them behind, he heard one of them pant, 'We gonna let an old fat guy get ahead of us?'

The teens sped up, one passing Scott on either side, both breathing harder than ever.

'Seeya, wouldn't want to be ya!' one of them puffed.

'Go with your bad selves,' Scott said, smiling.

He ran easily, eating up the road with long strides. Respiration still okay, ditto heart-rate, and why not? He was a hundred pounds lighter than he looked, and that was only half of what he had going for him. The other half was muscles still built for a man carrying 240.

Route 117 made a double curve, then ran straight beside Bowie Stream, babbling and chuckling along in its shallow, stony bed. Scott thought it had never sounded better, the misty air he was pulling deep into his lungs had never tasted better, the big pines crowding down on the other side of the road had never looked better. He could smell them, tangy and bright and somehow green. Every breath seemed deeper than the last, and he kept having to rein himself in.

I am so glad to be alive on this day, he thought.

Outside the covered bridge crossing the stream, one of those orange markers announced 6K. Beyond it was a sign reading HALFWAY HOME! The sound of feet thundering inside the bridge was — to Scott, at least — as beautiful as a Gene Krupa drumroll. Overhead, disturbed swallows raced back and forth under the roof. One actually flew into his face, its wing fluttering his brow, and he laughed aloud.

On the far side, one of the bike-shorts dudes was sitting on the guardrail, gasping for breath and massaging a cramp in his calf. He didn't look up as Scott and the other runners passed. At the junction of Routes 117 and 119, runners were clustered around a refreshment table, gulping water, Gatorade, and cranberry juice from paper cups before going on. Eight or nine others, who had blown themselves out on the first six kilometers, were sprawled on the grass. He was delighted to see Trevor Yount — the bullnecked Public Works guy with whom Scott had had the confrontation in Patsy's — was among them.

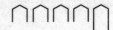

He passed the sign reading CASTLE ROCK MUNICIPAL TOWN LIMITS, where Route 119 became Bannerman Road, named after the town's longest serving sheriff, an unlucky fellow who had come to a bad end on one of the town's back roads. It was time to pick up the pace, and as Scott passed the orange 8K marker, he shifted from first gear to second. No problem. The air was cool and delicious on his blood-warmed skin, like being rubbed with silk, and he liked the feel of his own heart – that sturdy little engine – in his chest. There were houses on both sides of the road now, and people standing out on lawns, holding up signs and taking pictures.

Here was Milly Jacobs, still going but starting to slow down, her headband darkened to a deeper green with her sweat.

'How's that following wind, Milly? Picking any up?'

She turned to look at him, frankly incredulous. 'Good God, I can't . . . believe it's you,' she panted. 'Thought I left you . . . in the dust.'

'I found a little extra,' Scott said. 'Don't quit now, Milly, this is the good part.' Then she was behind him.

The road began to rise in a series of low but ascending hills, and Scott began to pass more runners – both those who had given up and those who were still laboring along. Two of the latter were the teenagers who had blown by him earlier, offended to be passed, even for a few moments, by a middle-aged fatty in shitty sneakers and old tennis shorts. They glanced at him with identical expressions of surprise. Smiling pleasantly, Scott said, 'Seeya, wouldn't want to be ya.'

One of them gave him the finger. Scott blew him a kiss, then showed them the heels of his shitty sneakers.

As Scott entered the ninth kilometer, a long peal of thunder rolled across the sky, west to east.

That's not good, he thought. November thunder might be okay in Louisiana, but not in Maine.

He came around a bend, jinking left to come even with a skinny old stork of a man who was running with his fists clenched before him and his head thrown back. His wifebeater shirt showed fishbelly white arms decorated with old tattoos. On his face he wore a daffy grin. 'You hear that thunder?'

'Yes!'

'Gonna rain a bitch! Ain't this a day?'

'You bet your ass,' Scott said, laughing. 'Finest kind!' Then he was past, but not before the skinny old guy gave him a pretty good swat on the ass.

The road ran straight now, and Scott spotted the red shirt and blue shorts halfway up Hunter's Hill, aka Runners' Heartbreak. He could see only half a dozen

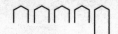

runners ahead of McComb now. There might already be a couple beyond the crest of the hill, but Scott doubted it.

It was time to shift into a higher gear.

He did so, and was now among the serious runners, the greyhounds. But many of them were either beginning to flag or saving their energy for the steep grade. He caught unbelieving looks as the middle-aged man with his belly pushing out his sweaty tee-shirt first wove his way among them, then put them behind him.

Partway up Hunter's Hill, Scott's breath began to shallow up, and the air going in and out began to taste hot and coppery. His feet no longer felt so light, and his calves were burning. There was a dull ache on the left side of his groin, as if he had strained something there. The second half of the hill looked endless. He thought about what Milly had said: first fun, then heck, then hell. Was he in heck or hell now? On the border, he decided.

He had never really assumed he could beat Deirdre McComb (although he hadn't discounted the possibility), but he *had* assumed he would finish the race somewhere near the front – that the muscles built to carry his earlier, heavier self would be enough to bring him through. Now, as he passed a couple of runners who had given up, one sitting with his head bent, the other lying on his back and gasping, he began to wonder about that.

Maybe I still weigh too much, he thought. Or maybe I just don't have the sack for this.

There was another roll of thunder.

Because the top of Hunter's didn't seem to be getting any closer, he looked down at the road, watching the pebbles set in the macadam flying past like galaxies in a science fiction movie. He looked up just in time to keep from crashing into a redhead who was standing with one foot on either side of the yellow line, holding onto her knees and gasping. Scott barely avoided her and saw the crest of the hill sixty yards ahead. Also one of those orange markers: 10K. He fixed his eyes on it and ran, now not just gasping for breath but *yanking* for it, and feeling every one of his forty-two years. His left knee began to complain, pulsing in sync with the pain in his groin. Sweat ran down his cheeks like hot water.

You are going to do this. You *will* do this. Put it all on the line.

And why the fuck not? If Zero Day turned out to be today instead of in February or March, so be it.

He passed the marker and crested the hill. Purdy's Lumberyard was on the right, Purdy's Hardware on the left. Just two klicks to go. He could see downtown

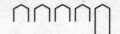

below him, twenty or so businesses on either side hung with bunting, the Catholic church and the Methodist one facing off like holy gunslingers, the slant parking (every space taken), the clogged sidewalks, and the town's two stoplights. Beyond the second one was the Tin Bridge, where bright yellow finishing tape decorated with turkeys had been strung. Ahead of Scott he now saw only six or seven runners. The one in the red shirt was second, and closing the distance on the leader. Deirdre was making her move.

I'm never going to catch her, Scott thought. She's got too much of a lead. That damn hill didn't break me, but it bent me pretty good.

Then his lungs seemed to open up again, each breath going deeper than the one before. His sneakers (not blinding white Adidas, just ratty old Pumas) seemed to shed the lead coating they had gained. His previous lightness of body came rushing back. It was what Milly had called the following wind, and what pros like McComb no doubt called the runner's high. Scott preferred that. He remembered that day in his yard, flexing his knees, leaping, and catching the branch of the tree. He remembered running up and down the bandstand steps. He remembered dancing across the kitchen floor as Stevie Wonder sang 'Superstition.' This was the same. Not a wind, not even a high, exactly, but an elevation. A sense that you had gone beyond yourself and could go farther still.

Heading down Hunter's, past O'Leary Ford on one side and Zoney's Go-Mart on the other, he passed one runner, then another. Four back now. He didn't know or care if they were staring as he blew past them. All of his attention was focused on the red shirt and blue shorts.

Deirdre took the lead. As she did, more thunder banged overhead – God's starter pistol – and Scott felt the first cold splat of rain on the back of his neck. Then another on his arm. He looked down and saw more hitting the road, darkening it in dime-sized drops. Now there were spectators on either side of Main, although they still had to be a mile from the finish and half a mile from where the downtown sidewalks started. Scott saw umbrellas popping open like flowers blooming. They were gorgeous. Everything was – the darkening sky, the pebbles in the road, the orange of the marker announcing the Turkey Trot's last K. The world stood forth.

Ahead of him, a runner abruptly swerved off the road, went to his knees, and rolled over on his back, looking up into the rain with his mouth drawn down in a bow of agony. Only two runners between him and Deirdre.

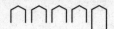

Scott blew past the final orange marker. Just a kilometer to go now, less than a mile. He had gone from first gear to second. Now, as the sidewalks began – cheering crowds on either side, some waving Turkey Trot pennants – it was time to see if he had not just third gear but an overdrive.

Kick it, you son of a bitch, he thought, and picked up the pace.

The rain seemed to hesitate for a moment, time enough for Scott to think it was going to hold off until the race was over, and then it came in a full-force torrent, driving the spectators back under awnings and into doorways. Visibility dropped to twenty percent, then to ten, then to almost zero. Scott thought the cold rain felt more than delicious; closer to divine.

He got by one runner, then another. The second was the former leader, the one that Deirdre had passed. He had slowed down to a walk, splashing along the gushing street with his head down, his hands on his hips, and his sopping shirt plastered to his body.

Ahead, through a gray curtain of rain, Scott saw the red shirt. He thought he had just enough gas left in the tank to go by her, but the race might be over before he could. The traffic light at the end of Main Street had disappeared. So had the Tin Bridge, and the yellow tape across its near end. It was just him and

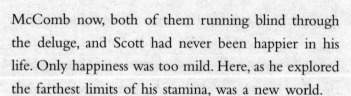

McComb now, both of them running blind through the deluge, and Scott had never been happier in his life. Only happiness was too mild. Here, as he explored the farthest limits of his stamina, was a new world.

Everything leads to this, he thought. To this elevation. If it's how dying feels, everyone should be glad to go.

He was close enough to see Deirdre McComb look back, her sodden ponytail doing a dead-fish flop onto her shoulder as she did it. Her eyes widened when she saw who was trying to take away her lead. She faced forward, lowered her head, and found more speed.

Scott first matched her, then overmatched her. Closing in, closing in, now almost close enough to touch the back of her soaked shirt, able to see clear rivulets of rain running down the back of her neck. Able – even over the roar of the storm – to hear her gasping air out of the rain. He could see her, but not the buildings they were passing on either side, or the last stoplight, or the bridge. He had lost all sense of where he was on Main, and had no landmarks to help him. His only landmark was the red shirt.

She looked back again, and that was a mistake. Her left foot caught her right ankle and she went down, arms out, surfing water up in front and splashing to either side like a kid bellyflopping into

a swimming pool. He heard her grunt as the air went out of her.

Scott reached her, stopped, bent down. She twisted up on one arm to look at him. Her face was an agony of fury and hurt. 'How did you cheat?' she gasped. 'Goddam you, how did you ch—'

He grabbed her. Lightning flashed, a brief glare that made him wince. 'Come on.' He put his other arm around her waist and hauled her up.

Her eyes went wide. There was another flash of lightning. 'Oh my God, what are you doing? *What's happening to me?*'

He ignored this. Her feet moved, but not on the street, which was now an inch deep in running water; they pedaled in the air. He knew what was happening to her, and he was sure it was amazing, but it wasn't happening to him. She was light to herself, maybe more than light, but heavy to him, a slim body that was all muscle and sinew. He let loose. He still couldn't see the Tin Bridge, but he could see a faint yellow streak that had to be the tape.

'*Go!*' he shouted, and pointed at the finish line. '*Run!*'

She did. He ran after her. She broke the tape. Lightning flashed. He followed, raising his hands into the rain, slowing down as he ran onto the Tin Bridge.

He found her halfway across on her hands and knees. He dropped down beside her, both of them gasping in air that seemed to be mostly liquid.

She looked at him, water running down her face like tears.

'What happened? My God, you put your arm around me and it was like I weighed nothing!'

Scott thought of the coins he had put in the pockets of his parka on the day he'd first gone to see Doctor Bob. He thought about standing on his bathroom scale while holding a pair of twenty-pound hand-weights.

'You did,' he said.

'DeeDee! *DeeDee!*'

It was Missy, running toward them. She held out her arms. Deirdre splashed to her feet and embraced her wife. They staggered and almost went down. Scott put his arms out to catch them, but didn't actually touch them. Lightning flashed.

Then the crowd found them, and they were surrounded by the people of Castle Rock, applauding in the rain.

CHAPTER 5

After the Race

THAT EVENING SCOTT WAS lying in a tub filled with water as hot as he could stand it, trying to soothe the ache out of his muscles. When his phone began to ring, he fumbled for it under the clean clothes folded on the chair by the tub. I'm tied to this damn thing, he thought.

'Hello?'

'Deirdre McComb, Mr Carey. What night shall I set aside for our dinner? Next Monday would be good, because the restaurant is closed on Mondays.'

Scott smiled. 'I think you misunderstood the wager, Ms McComb. You won, and your dogs now have free rein on my lawn, in perpetuity.'

'We both know that isn't exactly true,' she said. 'In fact, you threw the race.'

'You deserved to win.'

She laughed. It was the first one he'd heard from her, and it was charming. 'My high school running coach would tear his hair out if he heard such a sentiment. He used to say what you deserve has nothing to do with where you finish. I will take the win, however, if you invite us to dinner.'

'Then I'll brush up on my vegetarian cooking. Next Monday works for me, but only if you bring your wife. Sevenish, say?'

'That's fine, and she wouldn't miss it. Also . . .' She hesitated. 'I want to apologize for what I said. I know you didn't cheat.'

'No apology necessary,' Scott said, and he meant it. Because, in a way he had cheated, involuntary as it might have been.

'If not for that, I need to apologize for how I've treated you. I could plead extenuating circumstances,

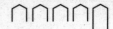

but Missy tells me there are none, and she might be right about that. I have certain . . . attitudes . . . and changing them hasn't been easy.'

He couldn't think of what to say to that, so he changed the subject. 'Are either of you gluten-free? Lactose-intolerant? Let me know, so I don't make something you or Missy – Ms Donaldson – can't eat.'

She laughed again. 'We don't eat meat or fish, and that's it. Everything else is on the table.'

'Even eggs?'

'Even eggs, Mr Carey.'

'Scott. Call me Scott.'

'I will. And I'm Deirdre. Or DeeDee, to avoid confusion with Dee the dog.' She hesitated. 'When we come to dinner, can you explain what happened when you pulled me up? I've had strange sensations while I'm running, strange perceptions, every runner will tell you the same—'

'I had a few myself,' Scott said. 'From Hunter's Hill on, things got very . . . weird.'

'But I've never felt anything like that. For a few seconds it was like I was on the space station, or something.'

'Yes, I can explain. But I'd like to invite my friend Dr Ellis, who already knows. And his wife, if she's available.' If she'll come, was what Scott didn't want to say.

'Fine. Until Monday, then. Oh, and be sure to look at the *Press-Herald*. The story won't be in the newspaper until tomorrow, of course, but it's online now.'

Sure it is, Scott thought. In the twenty-first century, print newspapers are also buggy-whip factories.

'I'll do that.'

'Did you think it was lightning? There at the end?'

'Yes,' Scott said. What else would it have been? Lightning went with thunder like peanut butter went with jelly.

'So did I,' DeeDee McComb said.

He dressed and fired up his computer. The story was on the *Press-Herald*'s homepage, and he was sure it would be on the front page of Saturday's paper, maybe above the fold, barring any new world crisis. The headline read: LOCAL RESTAURANT OWNER WINS CASTLE ROCK TURKEY TROT. According to the paper, it was the first time a town resident had won the race since 1989. There were only two photographs in the online edition, but Scott guessed there would be more in Saturday's print version. It hadn't been lightning at the end; it had been the newspaper photographer, and he'd gotten class-A pix despite the rain.

The first one showed Deirdre and Scott together, with the Tin Bridge stoplight a smeary red in the

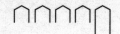

background, which meant she must have fallen not even seventy yards from the finish. He had his arm around her waist. Hair that had come loose from her ponytail was plastered to her cheeks. She was looking up at him with exhausted wonder. He was looking down at her . . . and smiling.

SHE GOT BY WITH A LITTLE HELP FROM A FRIEND, the caption read, and below that: *Fellow Castle Rocker Scott Carey helps Deirdre McComb to her feet after she took a spill on the wet road just short of the finish line.*

The second photo was captioned *VICTORY HUG*, and named the three people in the picture: Deirdre McComb, Melissa Donaldson, and Scott Carey. Deirdre and Missy were embracing. Although Scott hadn't actually touched them, only raised his arms and curled them around the women in an instinctive gesture to catch them if they fell, he looked like he was joining the hug.

The body of the story named the restaurant Deirdre McComb ran with 'her partner,' and quoted a review that had run in the paper back in August, calling the food 'veggie cuisine with Tex-Mex flair that has to be experienced; this is a trip worth making.'

Bill D. Cat had taken his usual position when Scott was at his desktop, perched on an endtable and watching his pet human with inscrutable green eyes.

'Tell you what, Bill,' Scott said. 'If that doesn't bring in customers, nothing will.'

He went into the bathroom and stepped on the scale. Its news didn't surprise him. He was down to 137. It might have been the day's exertions, but he didn't actually believe that. What he believed was that by booting his metabolism into a higher gear (and overdrive at the end), he had sped the process up even more.

It was starting to look like Zero Day might come weeks earlier than he had anticipated.

Myra Ellis did come to dinner with her husband. She was timid at first – almost skittish – and so was Missy Donaldson, but a glass of Pinot (which Scott served with cheese, crackers, and olives) loosened both ladies up. And then, a miracle – they discovered they were both mycologically inclined, and spent most of the meal talking about edible mushrooms.

'You know so much about them!' Myra exclaimed. 'May I ask if you went to culinary school?'

'I did. After I met DeeDee, but long before we were married. I went to ICE. That's—'

'The Institute of Culinary Education in New York!' Myra exclaimed. A few crumbs tumbled onto her frilly silk blouse. She didn't notice. 'It's famous! Oh my God, I'm so *jealous*!'

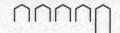

Deirdre was looking at them and smiling. Doctor Bob was, too. So that was good.

Scott had spent the morning at the local Hannaford's, with Nora's left-behind copy of *The Joy of Cooking* propped open in the child seat of his grocery cart. He asked many questions, and research paid off, as it usually did. He served vegetarian lasagna Florentine with garlic toast points. He was gratified – but not surprised – to see Deirdre put away not one or two but three big slices. She was still in post-run mode, and stuffing carbs.

'For dessert it's only store-bought pound cake,' he said, 'but the chocolate whipped cream I made myself.'

'I haven't had that since I was a kid,' Doctor Bob said. 'My mom made it for special occasions. We kids called it choco-cream. Bring it on, Scott.'

'Plus Chianti,' Scott said.

Deirdre applauded. She was flushed, her eyes sparkling, a woman with every part of her body clearly operating in top form. 'Bring that on, too!'

It was a fine meal, and the first time he'd pulled out all the stops in the kitchen since Nora had decamped. As he watched them eat and listened to them talk, he realized how empty this house had been with just him and Bill to ramble around in it.

The five of them demolished the pound cake. As Scott began to collect the plates, both Myra and Missy rose. 'Let us do that,' Myra said. 'You cooked.'

'Not at all, ma'am,' Scott said. 'I'm just going to put everything on the counter and load up the dishwasher later on.'

He took the dessert plates into the kitchen and stacked them on the counter. He turned and Deirdre was standing there, smiling.

'If you ever want a job, Missy's looking for a sous chef.'

'I don't think I could keep up with her,' Scott said, 'but I'll keep it in mind. How was business over the weekend? Must have been good if Missy's looking for help.'

'Sold out,' she said. 'Every table. People from away, but also people from the Rock that I've never seen before, at least not in our place. And we're booked solid for the next nine or ten days. This is like opening all over again, when people come to see what you've got. If what you've got isn't tasty, or even just so-so, most don't try again. But what Missy makes is a lot more than so-so. They *will* come back.'

'Winning the race made a difference, huh?'

'The *pictures* were what made the difference. And without you, the pictures would have just been a dyke winning a footrace, big deal.'

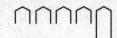

'You're too hard on yourself.'

She shook her head, smiling. 'I don't think so. Brace yourself, big boy, I'm coming in for a hug.'

She stepped forward. Scott stepped back, holding his hands out, palms forward. Her face clouded.

'It's not you,' he said. 'Believe me, I'd love nothing more than to hug you. We both deserve it. But it might not be safe.'

Missy was standing in the kitchen doorway with wineglasses held between her fingers by the stems. 'What is it, Scott? Is something wrong with you?'

He grinned. 'You might say.'

Doctor Bob joined the women. 'Are you going to tell them?'

'Yes,' Scott said. 'In the living room.'

He told them everything. The relief was enormous. Myra only looked puzzled, as if she hadn't quite taken it in, but Missy was disbelieving.

'It's not possible. People's bodies change when they lose weight, that's just a fact.'

Scott hesitated, then went to where she was sitting next to Deirdre on the couch. 'Give me your hand. Just for a second.'

She held it out with no hesitation. Total trust. This much can't hurt, he told himself, and hoped it was

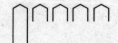

true. He had pulled Deirdre to her feet when she'd fallen, after all, and she was all right.

He took Missy's hand and pulled. She flew up from the couch, her hair streaming out behind her and her eyes wide. He caught her to keep her from crashing into him, lifted her, set her down, and stepped back. Her knees flexed when his hands left her and weight came back into her body. Then she stood, staring at him in amazement.

'You . . . I . . . *Jesus!*'

'What was it like?' Doctor Bob asked. He was sitting forward in his chair, eyes bright. 'Tell me!'

'It was . . . well . . . I don't think I can.'

'Try,' he urged.

'It was a little like being on a rollercoaster when it goes over the top of the first steep hill and starts down. My stomach went up . . .' She laughed shakily, still staring at Scott. '*Everything* went up!'

'I tried it with Bill,' Scott said, and nodded to where his cat was currently stretched out on the brick hearth. 'He freaked out. Laddered scratches up my arm in his hurry to jump down, and Bill never scratches.'

'Anything you take hold of has no weight?' Deirdre said. 'Is that really true?'

Scott thought about this. He had thought about it often, and sometimes it seemed to him that what was

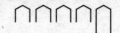

happening to him wasn't a phenomenon but something like a germ, or a virus.

'Living things have no weight. To *them*, at least, but—'

'They have weight to you.'

'Yes.'

'But other things? Inanimate objects?'

'Once I pick them up . . . or wear them . . . no. No weight.' He shrugged.

'How can that be?' Myra asked. 'How can that possibly be?' She looked at her husband. 'Do you know?'

He shook his head.

'How did it start?' Deirdre asked. 'What caused it?'

'No idea. I don't even know *when* it started, because I wasn't in the habit of weighing myself until the process was already under way.'

'In the kitchen you said it wasn't safe.'

'I said it might not be. I don't know for sure, but that sort of sudden weightlessness might screw up your heart . . . your blood-pressure . . . your brain function . . . who knows?'

'Astronauts are weightless,' Missy objected. 'Or almost. I guess those circling the earth must still be subject to at least some gravitational pull. And the ones who walked on the moon, as well.'

'It isn't just that, is it?' Deirdre said. 'You're afraid it might be contagious.'

Scott nodded. 'The idea has crossed my mind.'

There was a moment of silence, while all of them tried to digest the indigestible. Then Missy said, 'You have to go to a clinic! You have to be examined! Let the doctors who . . . who know about this sort of thing . . .'

She trailed off, recognizing the obvious: there were no doctors who knew about this sort of thing.

'They might be able to find a way to reverse it,' she said eventually. She turned to Ellis. 'You're a doctor. Tell him!'

'I have,' Doctor Bob said. 'Many times. Scott refuses. At first I thought that was wrong of him – wrong*headed* – but I've changed my mind. I doubt very much if this is something that can be scientifically investigated. It may stop on its own . . . even reverse itself . . . but I don't think the best doctors in the world could understand it, let alone affect it in any way, positive or negative.'

'And I have no desire to spend the remainder of my weight-loss program in a hospital room or a government facility, being examined,' Scott said.

'Or as a public curiosity, I suppose,' Deirdre said. 'I get that. Perfectly.'

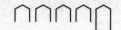

Scott nodded. 'So you'll understand when I ask you to promise that what's been said in this room has to stay in this room.'

'But what will happen to you?' Missy burst out. 'What will happen to you when you have no weight left?'

'I don't know.'

'How will you *live*? You can't just . . . just . . .' She looked around wildly, as if hoping for someone to finish her thought. No one did. 'You can't just float along the *ceiling*!'

Scott, who had already thought of a life like that, only shrugged again.

Myra Ellis leaned forward, her hands so tightly clasped the knuckles were white. 'Are you very frightened? I suppose you must be.'

'That's the thing,' Scott said. 'I'm not. I was at the very beginning, but now . . . I don't know . . . it seems sort of okay.'

There were tears in Deirdre's eyes, but she smiled. 'I think I get that, too,' she said.

'Yes,' he said. 'I believe you do.'

He thought that if any of them found it impossible to keep his secret, it would be Myra Ellis, with her church groups and committees. But she *did* keep it.

All of them did. They became a kind of cabal, getting together once a week at Holy Frijole, where Deirdre always kept a table reserved for them, with a little placard on it that said *Dr Ellis Party*. The place was always full, or nearly, and Deirdre said that after the new year, if things didn't slow down, they would have to open earlier and institute a second sitting. Missy had indeed hired a sous chef to help her in the kitchen, and on Scott's advice, she hired someone local – Milly Jacobs's oldest daughter.

'She's a little slow,' Missy said, 'but she's willing to learn, and by the time the summer people come back, she'll be fine. You'll see.'

Then she blushed and looked down at her hands, realizing Scott might not be around when the summer people came back.

On December 10th, Deirdre McComb lit the big Christmas tree in the Castle Rock town square. Almost a thousand people turned out for the evening ceremony, which included the high school chorus singing seasonal songs. Mayor Coughlin, dressed as Santa Claus, arrived by helicopter.

There was applause when Deirdre mounted the podium, and a roar of approval when she proclaimed the thirty-foot spruce as 'the best Christmas tree in the best town in New England.'

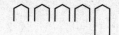

ELEVATION

The lights came on, the neon angel at the top twirled and curtseyed, and the crowd sang along with the high schoolers: Christmas tree, O Christmas tree, how lovely are your branches. Scott was amused to see Trevor Yount singing and applauding along with everyone else.

On that day, Scott Carey weighed 114 pounds.

CHAPTER 6

The Incredible Lightness of Being

THERE WERE LIMITS TO what Scott had come to think of as 'the weightless effect.' His clothes did not float up from his body. Chairs did not levitate when he sat in them, although if he carried one into the bathroom and stood on the scale with it, its weight didn't register.

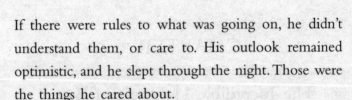

If there were rules to what was going on, he didn't understand them, or care to. His outlook remained optimistic, and he slept through the night. Those were the things he cared about.

He called Mike Badalamente on New Year's Day, passed on the appropriate good wishes, and then said he was thinking about making a trip to California in a few weeks, to see his only surviving aunt. If he made the trip, would Mike take his cat?

'Well, I don't know,' Mike said. 'Maybe. Does he do his business in a litter box?'

'Absolutely.'

'Why me?'

'Because I believe every bookstore should have a resident cat, which you are currently lacking.'

'How long are you planning to be gone?'

'Don't know. It sort of depends on how Aunt Harriet is doing.' There was no Aunt Harriet, of course, and he would have to have Doctor Bob or Myra take the cat to Mike's. Deirdre and Missy both smelled of dog, and Scott could no longer even stroke his old friend; Bill ran away if he came too near.

'What does he eat?'

'Friskies,' Scott said. 'And a good supply will come with the animal. If I decide to go, that is.'

'Okay, you got a deal.'

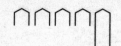

'Thanks, Mike. You're a pal.'

'I am, but not just because of that. You did this town a small but valuable mitzvah when you helped the McComb woman get up so she could finish the race. What was happening with her and her wife was ugly. It's better now.'

'A *little* better.'

'Actually quite a lot.'

'Well, thanks. And Happy New Year again.'

'Back atcha, buddy. What's the feline's name?'

'Bill. Bill D. Cat, actually.'

'Like in *Bloom County*. Cool.'

'Pick him up and give him a stroke once in awhile. If I decide to go, that is. He likes that.'

Scott hung up, thought about what giving things away meant – especially things that were also valued friends – and closed his eyes.

Doctor Bob called a few days later, and asked Scott if his weight-loss was remaining constant at one and a half to two pounds a day. Scott said it was, knowing the lie couldn't come back to haunt him; he looked the same as ever, right down to the bulge of belly hanging over his belt.

'So . . . you still think you'll be down to nothing in early March?'

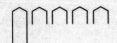

'Yes.'

Scott now thought Zero Day might come before January was out, but he didn't know for sure, couldn't even make an educated guess, because he had stopped weighing himself. Not so long ago he had avoided the bathroom scale because it showed too many pounds; now he stayed away for the opposite reason. The irony was not lost on him.

For the time being Bob and Myra Ellis were not to know how things had speeded up, nor were Missy and Deirdre. He would have to tell them eventually, because when the end came, he would need help from one of them. And he knew which one.

'What do you weigh now?' Doctor Bob asked.

'106,' Scott said.

'Holy shit!'

He guessed Ellis would say a lot more than holy shit if he knew what Scott knew: it was more like seventy. He could cross his big living room in four loping strides, or jump, catch one of the overhead beams, and swing from it like Tarzan. He hadn't reached what his weight would be on the moon, but he was closing in on it.

Doctor Bob was silent for a moment, then said, 'Have you considered that the cause of what's happening to you might be alive?'

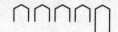

'Sure,' Scott said. 'Maybe an exotic bacteria that got into a cut, or some extremely rare virus that I inhaled.'

'Has it crossed your mind that it might be sentient?'

It was Scott's turn to be silent. At last he said, 'Yes.'

'You're dealing with this extremely well, I must say.'

'So far, so good,' Scott said, but three days later he discovered just how much he might have to deal with before the end came. You thought you knew, you thought you could get ready . . . and then you tried to get the mail.

Western Maine had been experiencing a January thaw since New Year's Day, with temperatures in the fifties. Two days after Doctor Bob's call, it climbed all the way into the sixties, and the kids went back to school wearing their light jackets. That night, however, temperatures dropped and a sleety, granular snow began falling.

Scott barely noticed. He spent the evening on his computer, ordering stuff. He could have gotten all the items locally – the wheelchair and chest harness from the ostomy department of the CVS where he'd bought his Halloween candy, the ramp and clamps from Purdy's Hardware – but local people had a tendency to talk. And ask questions. He didn't want that.

The snow ended around midnight, and the following day dawned clear and cold. The new snow, frozen to

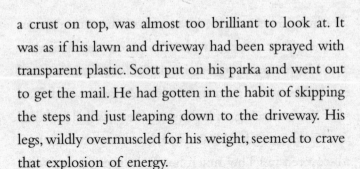

a crust on top, was almost too brilliant to look at. It was as if his lawn and driveway had been sprayed with transparent plastic. Scott put on his parka and went out to get the mail. He had gotten in the habit of skipping the steps and just leaping down to the driveway. His legs, wildly overmuscled for his weight, seemed to crave that explosion of energy.

He did it now, and when his feet hit the icy crust, they shot out from under him. He landed on his ass, started to laugh, then stopped when he began to slide. He went down the slope of the lawn on his back, like a weight along the sawdusty surface of an arcade bowling game, gaining speed as he approached the street. He grabbed at a bush, but it was coated with ice and his hand slid off. He rolled over on his stomach and spread his legs, thinking that might slow him down. It didn't. He only slued sideways.

The crust is thick but not *that* thick, he thought. If I weighed as much as I look like I weigh, I'd break through and stop. But I don't. I'm going into the street, and if a car's coming along, it probably won't be able to stop in time. Then I won't have to worry about Zero Day.

He didn't go that far. He struck the post on which his mailbox was mounted, and hard enough to knock the wind out of him. When he recovered, he tried to stand up. He did a split on the slippery crust and went

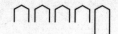

down again. He braced his feet against the post and pushed. That didn't work, either. He went four or five feet, his momentum died, and he slid back into the post. Next he tried pulling himself along, but his clutching fingers only slid on the crust. He had forgotten his gloves, and his hands were going numb.

I need help, he thought, and the name that immediately jumped to mind was Deirdre's. He reached into the pocket of his parka, but for once he had forgotten his phone. It was sitting back on his study desk. He supposed he could push himself into the street anyway, work his way over to the side, and wave down an oncoming car. Someone would stop and help him, but that someone would ask questions Scott didn't want to answer. His driveway was even more hopeless; it looked like a skating rink.

So here I am, he thought, like a turtle on its back. Hands going numb, feet soon to follow.

He craned to look up at the bare trees, their branches swaying mildly against the cloudless blue sky. He looked at the mailbox, and saw what might be a solution to his serio-comic problem. He sat up with his crotch braced against the post and grabbed the metal flag on the side of the box. It was loose, and two hard pulls was enough to snap it off. He used the ragged metal end to dig two holes in the crust. He put his knee in

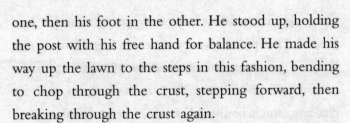

one, then his foot in the other. He stood up, holding the post with his free hand for balance. He made his way up the lawn to the steps in this fashion, bending to chop through the crust, stepping forward, then breaking through the crust again.

A couple of cars went by, and someone honked. Scott raised a hand and waved without turning around. By the time he got back to the steps, his hands had lost all feeling, and one was bleeding in two places. His back hurt like a motherfucker. He started up to the door, slipped, and barely managed to grab the ice-coated iron railing before he could go sliding back down to the mailbox again. He wasn't sure he would have had it in him to climb back up, even with holes to step in. He was exhausted, stinking with sweat inside his parka. He lay down in the hall. Bill came to look at him – but not *too* close – and miaowed his concern.

'I'm okay,' he said. 'Don't worry, you'll still get fed.'

Yes, I'm okay, he thought. Just a little impromptu sledding on the crust. But this is where the really weird shit begins.

He supposed if there was a consolation, it was that the really weird shit wouldn't last long.

But I need to put up those clamps and put down that ramp ASAP. Not much time now.

*

ELEVATION

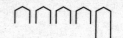

On a Monday evening in mid-month, the members of the 'Dr Ellis party' had their last meal together. Scott hadn't seen any of them for a week, citing the need to hole up and finish his current department store project. Which had actually been done, at least in first draft, before Christmas. He guessed someone else would be applying the finishing touches.

He said it would have to be a potluck, with them bringing the food, because cooking had become difficult for him. In truth, everything had become difficult. Going upstairs was easy enough; three large, effortless leaps did the job. Going down was harder. He was afraid he might tumble and break a leg, so he held the railing and eased down step by step, like an old man with gout and bad hips. He had also developed a tendency to run into walls, because momentum had become hard to judge and even harder to control.

Myra asked him about the ramp now covering the steps to the stoop. Doctor Bob and Missy were more concerned about the wheelchair sitting in the corner of the living room, and the chest harness – made for people with little or no ability to sit upright – draped over its back. Deirdre asked no questions, only looked at him with wise, unhappy eyes.

They ate a tasty vegetarian casserole (Missy), au gratin potatoes with a cheesy sauce (Myra), and topped

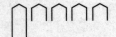

the meal off with a lumpy but tasty angel food cake that was only slightly burned on the bottom (Doctor Bob). The wine was good, but the talk and the laughter were better.

When they were finished, he said: 'Time to fess up. I've been lying to you. This has been going quite a bit faster than I said it was.'

'Scott, no!' Missy cried.

Doctor Bob nodded, seeming unsurprised. 'How much faster?'

'Three pounds a day, not one or two.'

'And how much do you weigh now?'

'I don't know. I've been avoiding the scale. Let's find out.'

Scott tried to stand. His thighs connected with the table and he flew forward, knocking over two wineglasses when he put out his hands to stop himself. Deirdre quickly picked up the tablecloth and threw it over the spill.

'Sorry, sorry,' Scott said. 'Don't know my own strength these days.'

He turned as gingerly as a man on roller skates, and started toward the back half of the house. No matter how carefully he tried to walk, his steps became leaps. His remaining weight wanted him on the earth; his muscles insisted he rise above it. He

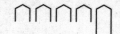

overbalanced and had to grab one of the newly installed clamps to keep from going headlong into the hallway.

'Oh God,' Deirdre said. 'It must be like learning to walk all over again.'

You should have seen the last time I tried to get the mail, Scott thought. That was a *real* learning experience.

At least none of them were revisiting the clinic idea. Not that their failure to do that surprised him. A single look at his locomotion, at once awkward, ridiculous, and weirdly graceful, was enough to dispel the idea that a clinic might do him any good. This was a private matter now. They understood that. He was glad.

They all crowded into the bathroom and watched him stand on the Ozeri scale. 'Jesus,' Missy said quietly. 'Oh, Scott.'

The readout was 30.2 pounds.

He made his way back to the dining room with them following along behind. He went as carefully as a man using stones to cross a creek, and still ended up running into the table again. Missy instinctively reached out to steady him, but he waved her off before she could touch him.

When they were seated, he said, 'I'm all right with this. Fine, in fact. Really.'

Myra was very pale. 'How can you be?'

'I don't know. I just am. But this is our farewell dinner. I won't see you guys again. Except for Deirdre. I need someone to help me at the end. Will you do it?'

'Yes, of course.' She didn't hesitate, only put an arm around her wife, who had begun to cry.

'I just want to say . . .' Scott stopped, cleared his throat. 'I want to say that I wish we had more time. You've been good friends to me.'

'There's no compliment more sincere than that,' Doctor Bob said. He was wiping his eyes with a napkin.

'It's not *fair*!' Missy burst out. 'It's not goddam *fair*!'

'Well, no,' Scott agreed, 'it isn't. But I'm not leaving any kids behind, my ex is happy where she is, there's that, and it's fairer than cancer, or Alzheimer's, or being a burn victim in a hospital ward. I guess I'd go down in history, if anyone talked about it.'

'Which we won't,' Doctor Bob said.

'No,' Deirdre agreed. 'We won't. Can you tell me what it is you need me to do, Scott?'

He could and did, mentioning everything except what was tucked away in a paper bag in the hall closet. They listened in silence, and no one spoke a word of disagreement.

When he finished, Myra asked, very timidly, 'What does it feel like, Scott? What do *you* feel like?'

Scott thought of how he'd felt running down Hunter's Hill, when he'd gotten his second wind and the whole world had stood revealed in the usually hidden glory of ordinary things – the leaden, lowering sky, the bunting flapping from the downtown buildings, every precious pebble and cigarette butt and beer can discarded by the side of the road. His own body for once working at top capacity, every cell loaded with oxygen.

'Elevated,' he said at last.

He looked at Deirdre McComb, saw her shining eyes fixed on his face, and knew she understood why he had chosen her.

Myra coaxed Bill into his cat carrier. Doctor Bob took it down to his 4Runner and stowed it in the back. Then the four of them stood on the porch, their breath pluming in the cold night air. Scott remained in the entry, holding tight to one of the clamps.

'May I say something before we go?' Myra asked.

'Of course,' Scott said, but wished she wouldn't. He wished they would just leave. He thought he had discovered one of life's great truths (and one he could have done without): the only thing harder

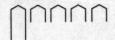

than saying goodbye to yourself, a pound at a time, was saying goodbye to your friends.

'I was very foolish. I'm sorry about what's happening to you, Scott, but I'm glad about what's happened to me. If it hadn't, I would have stayed blind to some very good things, and some very good people. I would have stayed a foolish old woman. I can't hug you, so this will have to do.'

She opened her arms, drew Deirdre and Missy to her, and embraced them. They hugged her back.

Doctor Bob said, 'If you need me, I'll come at a sprint.' He laughed. 'Well, no, my sprinting days are actually behind me, but you know what I mean.'

'I do,' Scott said. 'Thank you.'

'So long, old man. Take care where you step. And how.'

Scott watched them walk to Doctor Bob's car. He watched them get in. He waved, being careful to hold onto the clamp as he did it. Then he closed the door and made his half-walking, half-leaping way to the kitchen, feeling like a cartoon character. Which was, at bottom, the reason it felt so important to keep this a secret. He was sure he looked absurd, and it *was* absurd . . . but only if you were on the outside.

He sat down at the kitchen counter and looked at the empty corner where Bill's food and water dish had

been for the last seven years. He looked at it for a long time. Then he went up to bed.

The following day, he got an email from Missy Donaldson.

I told DeeDee I wanted to go with her, and be there at the end. We had quite an argument about it, I didn't give in until she reminded me about my foot, and how I felt about it when I was a young girl. I can run now – I love to run – but I was never a competition runner like DeeDee, because I'm only good for short distances, even after all these years. I was born with talipes equinovarus, you see, which is more commonly known as clubfoot. I had surgery to correct it when I was seven years old, but until then I walked with a cane, and it took me years afterward to learn to walk normally.

When I was four – I remember this very clearly – I showed my foot to my friend Felicity. She laughed and said it was a gross-ugly stupid foot. After that I didn't let anyone look at it except for my mother and the doctors. I didn't want people to laugh. DeeDee says that's how you feel about what's happening to you. She said, 'He wants you to remember him the way he was when he was normal, not bouncing around

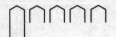

in his house and looking like a bad special effect from a 1950s sci-fi movie.'

Then I got it, but that doesn't mean I like it, or that you deserve it.

Scott, what you did the day of the race made it possible for us to stay in Castle Rock, not just because we have a business here but because now we can be a part of the town's greater life. DeeDee thinks she is going to be invited to join the Jaycees. She laughs and says it's silly, but I know that inside she doesn't think it's silly at all. It's a trophy, the same as the ones she got in the races she won. Oh, not everyone will accept us, I'm not so silly (or naive) as to believe that, some will never come around, but most will. Many already have. Without you that never would have happened, and without you, part of my beloved would always have remained closed off to the world. She won't tell you this, but I will: you knocked the chip off her shoulder. It was a big chip, and now she can walk straight again. She's always been a prickly pear, and I don't expect that to change, but she's open now. She sees more, hears more, can be more. You made that possible. You picked her up when she fell.

She says there's a bond between you, a shared feeling, and that's why she has to be the one to help

you at the end. Am I jealous? A little, but I think I understand. It was when you said you felt elevated. She is that way when she runs. It's why she runs.

Please be brave, Scott, and please know I am thinking of you. God bless.

All my love,
Missy

PS: When we go to the bookstore, we'll always pet Bill.

Scott thought about calling her and thanking her for saying such kind things, then decided that was a bad idea. It might get them both going. He printed out her note instead, and put it in one of the pockets of the harness.

He would take it with him when he went.

The following Sunday morning, Scott went along the hall to the downstairs bathroom in a series of steps that weren't steps at all. Each one was a long float that took him up to the ceiling, where he would push his tented fingers to bring himself back down. The furnace kicked on, and the soft whoosh of air from the vent actually blew him sideways a little. He twisted and grabbed a clamp to pull himself past the draft.

In the bathroom, he hovered over the scale and finally settled. At first he thought it wasn't going to report any weight at all. Then, at last, it coughed up a number: 2.1. It was about what he had expected.

That evening he called Deirdre's cell. He kept it simple. 'I need you. Can you come?'

'Yes.' It was all she said, and all he needed.

The door of the house was shut but unlocked. Deirdre slipped in, not opening the door all the way because of the draft. She turned on the hall lights to dispel the shadows, then went into the living room. Scott was in the wheelchair. He had managed to get partway into the harness, which had been buckled to the back of the chair, but his body floated upward from the chair's seat and one arm hung in the air. His face was bright with sweat, the front of his shirt dark with it.

'I almost waited too long,' he said. He sounded breathless. 'I had to swim down to the chair. Breaststroke, if you can believe it.'

Deirdre could. She went to him and stood in front of the wheelchair, looking at him with wonder. 'How long have you been here like this?'

'Awhile. Wanted to wait until dark. *Is* it dark?'

'Almost.' She dropped to her knees. 'Oh, Scott. This is so bad.'

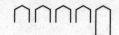

He shook his head back and forth in slow motion, like a man shaking his head underwater. 'You know better.'

She thought she did. Hoped she did.

He struggled with his floating arm and finally managed to shoot it into the vest's armhole. 'Can you try to buckle the straps across my chest and waist without touching me?'

'I think so,' she said, but twice her knuckles brushed him as she knelt in front of the chair – once his side, once his shoulder – and both times she felt her body rise and then settle back. Her stomach did a flip with each contact, what she remembered her father calling a whoops-my-dear when their car went over a big bump. Or, yes – Missy had been right – like when a rollercoaster crested the first hill, hesitated, then plunged.

At last it was done. 'Now what?'

'Soon we sample the night air. But first go into the closet, the one in the entry where I keep my boots. There's a paper bag, and a coil of rope. I think you can push the wheelchair, but if you can't, you'll have to tie the rope around the headrest and pull it.'

'And you're sure about this?'

He nodded, smiling. 'Do you think I want to spend the rest of my life tied into this thing? Or having someone climb a stepladder to feed me?'

'Well, that would make a dandy YouTube video.'

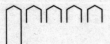

'One no one would believe.'

She found the rope and the brown paper bag and took them back to the living room. Scott held out his hands. 'Come on, big girl, let's see your skills. Toss me the bag from there.'

She did, and it was a good throw. The bag arced through the air toward his outreached hands . . . stopped less than an inch above his palms . . . then settled slowly into them. There the bag seemed to gain weight, and Deirdre had to remind herself of what he'd said when he first explained what was happening: things were heavy to *him*. Was that a paradox? It made her head hurt, whatever it was, and there was no time to think about it now, anyway. He stripped off the paper bag and held a square object wrapped in thick paper decorated with starbursts. Protruding from the bottom was a flat red tongue about six inches long.

'It's called a SkyLight. A hundred and fifty dollars from Fireworks Factory in Oxford. I bought it online. Hope it's worth it.'

'How will you light it? How can you, when . . . when you're . . .'

'Don't know if I can, but confidence is high. It's got a scratch fuse.'

'Scott, do I have to do this?'

'Yes,' he said.

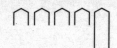

'You want to go.'

'Yes,' he said. 'It's time.'

'It's cold outside, and you're covered with sweat.'

'It doesn't matter.'

But it did to her. She went upstairs to his bedroom and pulled the comforter off a bed that had been slept in – at some point, anyway – but bore no impression of his body on the mattress or his head on the pillow.

'Comforter,' she snorted. It seemed a very stupid word under the circumstances. She took it downstairs and tossed it to him as she had tossed the paper bag, watching with the same fascination as it paused . . . bloomed . . . and then settled over his chest and lap.

'Wrap that around you.'

'Yes, ma'am.'

She watched him do it, then tucked the part trailing on the floor under his feet. This time the lift was more serious, the whoops-my-dear a double flip instead of a single. Her knees rose from the floor and she could feel her hair stream upward. Then it was done, and when her knees thumped down on the boards again, she had a better understanding of why he could smile. She remembered something she'd read in college – Faulkner, maybe: *Gravity is the anchor that pulls us down into our graves*. There would be no grave for this man, and no more gravity, either. He had been given a special dispensation.

'Snug as a bug in a rug,' he said.

'Don't joke, Scott. Please.'

She went behind the wheelchair and put her hands tentatively on the jutting handles. There was no need of the rope; her weight stayed. She pushed him toward the door, onto the stoop, and down the ramp.

The night was cold, chilling the sweat on his face, but the air was as sweet and crisp as the first bite of a fall apple. Above him was a half-moon and what seemed like a trillion stars.

To match the trillion pebbles, just as mysterious, that we walk over every day, he thought. Mystery above, mystery below. Weight, mass, reality: mystery all around.

'Don't you cry,' he said. 'This isn't a goddam funeral.'

She pushed him onto the snowy lawn. The wheels sank eight inches deep and stopped. Not far from the house, but far enough to avoid being caught under one of the eaves. That *would* be an anticlimax, he thought, and laughed.

'What's the joke, Scott?'

'Nothing,' he said. 'Everything.'

'Look down there. At the street.'

Scott saw three bundled-up figures, each with a flashlight: Missy, Myra, and Doctor Bob.

'I couldn't keep them away.' Deirdre came around

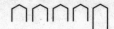

the wheelchair and dropped to one knee in front of the bundled-up figure with his bright eyes and sweat-clumped hair.

'Did you try? Tell the truth, DeeDee.' It was the first time he had called her that.

'Well . . . not very hard.'

He nodded and smiled. 'Good discussion.'

She laughed, then wiped her eyes. 'Are you ready?'

'Yes. Can you help me with the buckles?'

She managed the two holding the harness to the back of the chair, and he rose at once against the lap strap. She had to struggle with that, because it was tight and her hands were going numb in the January cold. She kept touching him, and each time she did her body would rise from the snow cover, making her feel like a human pogo stick. She stuck with it, and finally the last strap holding him to the chair began to slide free.

'I love you, Scott,' she said. 'We all do.'

'Right back atcha,' he said. 'Give your good girl a kiss for me.'

'Two,' she promised.

Then the strap slithered out of the buckle and it was done.

He rose slowly from the chair, the coverlet trailing below him like the hem of a long skirt, feeling absurdly like

Mary Poppins, minus the umbrella. Then a breeze caught him, and he began to rise faster. He clutched the coverlet with one hand and the SkyLight against his chest with the other. He saw the diminishing circle of Deirdre's upturned face. He watched her wave, but his hands were occupied and he couldn't wave back. He saw the others wave from where they stood on View Drive. He saw their flashlights focused on him, and noted how they began drawing together as he gained altitude.

The breeze tried to turn him, making him think of how he'd slued sideways on his ridiculous trip down his snow-crusted lawn to the mailbox, but when he partially unwrapped the coverlet and held it out on the side the wind was coming from, he steadied. That might not last long, but it didn't matter. For the time being he only wanted to look down and see his friends – Deirdre on the lawn by the wheelchair, the others in the street. He passed his bedroom window and saw the lamp was still on, casting a yellow stripe on his bed. He could see things on his bureau – watch, comb, little fold of money – that he would never touch again. He rose higher, and the moonlight was bright enough for him to see some kid's Frisbee caught in an angle of the roof, maybe tossed up there before he and Nora had bought the place.

That kid could be grown up now, he thought. Writing in New York or digging ditches in San

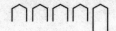

Francisco or painting in Paris. Mystery, mystery, mystery.

Now he caught escaping heat from the house, a thermal, and began rising faster. The town disclosed itself as if from a drone or low-flying plane, the street-lamps along Main Street and Castle View like pearls on a string. He could see the Christmas tree that Deirdre had lit over a month ago, and which would remain in the town square until the first of February.

It was cold up here, much colder than on the ground, but that was all right. He let the coverlet go and watched it drop, spreading out as it went, slowing, becoming a parachute, not weightless but almost.

Everyone should have this, he thought, and perhaps, at the end, everyone does. Perhaps in their time of dying, everyone rises.

He held out the SkyLight and scratched the fuse with a fingernail. Nothing happened.

Light, damn you. I didn't get much of a last meal, so could I at least have a last wish?

He scratched again.

'I can't see him anymore,' Missy said. She was crying. 'He's gone. We might as well—'

'Wait,' Deirdre said. She had joined them at the foot of Scott's driveway.

'For what?' Doctor Bob asked.

'Just wait.'

So they waited, looking up into the darkness.

'I don't think—' Myra began.

'A little longer,' Deirdre said, thinking, Come on, Scott, come on, you're almost at the finish line, it's your race to win, your tape to break through, so don't blow it. Don't choke. Come on, big boy, let's see your skills.

Brilliant fire burst high above them: reds and yellows and greens. There was a pause, then came a perfect fury of gold, a shimmering waterfall that rained down and rained down and rained down, as if it would never end.

Deirdre took Missy's hand.

Doctor Bob took Myra's hand.

They watched until the last golden sparks went out, and the night was dark again. Somewhere high above them, Scott Carey continued to gain elevation, rising above the earth's mortal grip with his face turned toward the stars.

Don't miss THE INSTITUTE by Stephen King

**Thrilling, suspenseful, heartbreaking,
THE INSTITUTE is a stunning novel of
childhood betrayed and hope regained.**

Luke Ellis, a super-smart twelve-year-old with an
exceptional gift, is the latest in a long line of kids
abducted and taken to a secret government facility,
hidden deep in the forest in Maine.

Here, kids who can read minds or make objects move are
subjected to a series of experiments. There seems to be
no hope of escape. Until Luke teams up with an even
younger boy whose powers of telepathy are off the scale,
and they create a plan.

Meanwhile, far away in a small town in South Carolina,
former cop Tim Jamieson has taken a job working for
the local sheriff. Tim is just walking the beat. The quiet
life. He doesn't know he's about to take on the biggest
case of his career . . .

Turn the page for an excerpt . . .

First published in Great Britain in 2019 by Hodder & Stoughton
An Hachette UK company

1

Grateful acknowledgement is made for permission to reprint
excerpts from the following copyrighted material:

ROAD RUNNER
Words and Music by BARBARA CAMERON © 1972
(Renewed) WB MUSIC CORP.
All rights reserved. Used by permission of ALFRED PUBLISHING, LLC

'I Shall Be Released'
Written by Bob Dylan
Copyright © 1967, 1970 by Dwarf Music; renewed 1995 by Dwarf Music.
All rights reserved. International copyright secured. Reprinted by permission

A CIP catalogue record for this title is available from the British Library

Hardback ISBN 978 1 529 35539 0
Trade Paperback ISBN 978 1 529 35540 6
eBook ISBN 978 1 529 35542 0

Typeset in Bembo by Palimpsest Book Production Ltd, Falkirk, Stirlingshire

Printed and bound in Great Britain by Clays Ltd, Elcograf S.p.A.

Hodder & Stoughton policy is to use papers that are natural, renewable
and recyclable products and made from wood grown in sustainable forests.
The logging and manufacturing processes are expected to conform to
the environmental regulations of the country of origin.

Hodder & Stoughton Ltd
Carmelite House
50 Victoria Embankment
London EC4Y 0DZ

www.hodder.co.uk

According to the National Center for Missing and Exploited Children, roughly 800,000 children are reported missing each year in the United States. Most are found.
Thousands are not.

THE NIGHT KNOCKER

1

Half an hour after Tim Jamieson's Delta flight was scheduled to leave Tampa for the bright lights and tall buildings of New York, it was still parked at the gate. When a Delta agent and a blond woman with a security badge hanging around her neck entered the cabin, there were unhappy, premonitory murmurings from the packed residents of economy class.

'May I have your attention, please!' the Delta guy called.

'How long's the delay gonna be?' someone asked. 'Don't sugarcoat it.'

'The delay should be short, and the captain wants to assure you all that your flight will arrive approximately on time. We have a federal officer who needs to board, however, so we'll need someone to give up his or her seat.'

A collective groan went up, and Tim saw several people unlimber their cell phones in case of trouble. There had been trouble in these situations before.

'Delta Air Lines is authorized to offer a free ticket to New York on the next outbound flight, which will be tomorrow morning at 6:45 AM—'

Another groan went up. Someone said, 'Just shoot me.'

The functionary continued, undeterred. 'You'll be given a hotel voucher for tonight, plus four hundred dollars. It's a good deal, folks. Who wants it?'

He had no takers. The security blond said nothing, only surveyed the crowded economy-class cabin with all-seeing but somehow lifeless eyes.

'Eight hundred,' the Delta guy said. 'Plus the hotel voucher and the complimentary ticket.'

'Guy sounds like a quiz show host,' grunted a man in the row ahead of Tim's.

There were still no takers.

'Fourteen hundred?'

And still none. Tim found this interesting but not entirely surprising. It wasn't just because a six forty-five flight meant getting up before God, either. Most of his fellow economy-class passengers were family groups headed home after visiting various Florida attractions, couples sporting beachy-keen sunburns, and beefy, red-faced, pissed-off-looking guys who probably had business in the Big Apple worth considerably more than fourteen hundred bucks.

Someone far in the back called, 'Throw in a Mustang convertible and a trip to Aruba for two, and you can have both our seats!' This sally provoked laughter. It didn't sound terribly friendly.

The gate agent looked at the blond with the badge, but if he hoped for help there, he got none. She just continued her survey, nothing moving but her eyes. He sighed and said, 'Sixteen hundred.'

Tim Jamieson suddenly decided he wanted to get the fuck off this plane and hitchhike north. Although such an idea had never so much as crossed his mind before this moment, he found he could imagine himself doing it, and with absolute clarity. There he was, standing on Highway 301 somewhere in the middle of Hernando County with his thumb out. It was hot, the lovebugs were swarming, there was a billboard advertising some slip-and-fall attorney, 'Take It on the Run' was blaring from a boombox sitting on the concrete-block step of a nearby trailer where a shirtless man was washing his car, and eventually some Farmer John would come along and give him a ride in a pickup truck with stake sides, melons in the back, and a magnetic Jesus on the dashboard. The best part wouldn't even be the cash money in his pocket. The best part would be standing out there by himself, miles from this sardine can with its warring smells of perfume, sweat, and hair spray.

The second-best part, however, would be squeezing the government tit for a few dollars more.

He stood up to his perfectly normal height (five-ten and a fraction), pushed his glasses up on his nose, and raised his hand. 'Make it two thousand, sir, plus a cash refund of my ticket, and the seat is yours.'

2

The voucher turned out to be for a cheesedog hotel located near the end of Tampa International's most heavily used runway. Tim fell asleep to the sound of airplanes, awoke to more of the same, and went down to ingest a hardboiled egg and two rubber pancakes from the complimentary breakfast buffet. Although far from a gourmet treat, Tim ate heartily, then went back to his room to wait for nine o'clock, when the banks opened.

He cashed his windfall with no trouble, because the bank knew he was coming and the check had been approved in advance; he had no intention of waiting around in the cheesedog hotel for it to clear. He took his two thousand in fifties and twenties, folded it into his left front pocket, reclaimed his duffel bag from the bank's security guard, and called an Uber to take him to Ellenton. There he paid the driver, strolled to the nearest 301-N sign, and stuck out his thumb. Fifteen minutes later he was picked up by an old guy in a Case gimme cap. There were no melons in the back of his pickup, and no stake sides, but otherwise it pretty much conformed to his vision of the previous night.

'Where you headed, friend?' the old guy asked.

'Well,' Tim said, 'New York, eventually. I guess.'

The old guy spat a ribbon of tobacco juice out the window. 'Now why would any man in his right mind want to go there?' He pronounced it *raht mahnd*.

'I don't know,' Tim said, although he did; an old service buddy had told him there was plenty of private security work in the Big Apple, including some for companies that would give more weight to his experience than to the

Rube Goldberg fuckup that had ended his career in Florida policing. 'I'm just hoping to get to Georgia tonight. Maybe I'll like that better.'

'Now you're talking,' the old guy said. 'Georgia ain't bad, specially if you like peaches. They gi' me the backdoor trots. You don't mind some music, do you?'

'Not at all.'

'Got to warn you, I play it loud. I'm a little on the deef side.'

'I'm just happy to be riding.'

It was Waylon Jennings instead of REO Speedwagon, but that was okay with Tim. Waylon was followed by Shooter Jennings and Marty Stuart. The two men in the mud-streaked Dodge Ram listened and watched the highway roll. Seventy miles up the line, the old guy pulled over, gave Tim a tip of his Case cap, and wished him a real fahn day.

Tim didn't make Georgia that night – he spent it in another cheesedog motel next to a roadside stand selling orange juice – but he got there the following day. In the town of Brunswick (where a certain kind of tasty stew had been invented), he took two weeks' work in a recycling plant, doing it with no more forethought than he had put into deciding to give up his seat on the Delta flight out of Tampa. He didn't need the money, but it seemed to Tim that he needed the time. He was in transition, and that didn't happen overnight. Also, there was a bowling alley with a Denny's right next door. Hard to beat a combo like that.

3

With his pay from the recycling plant added to his airline windfall, Tim was standing on the Brunswick ramp of I-95 North and feeling pretty well-heeled for a rambling man. He stood there for over an hour in the sun, and was thinking of giving up and going back to Denny's for a cold glass of sweet tea when a Volvo station wagon pulled over. The back was filled with cartons. The elderly woman behind the wheel powered down the passenger side window and peered at him through thick glasses. 'Although not large, you look well-muscled,' she said. 'You are not a rapist or a psychotic, are you?'

'No, ma'am,' Tim told her, thinking: But what else *would* I say?

'Of course you would say that, wouldn't you? Are you going as far as South Carolina? Your duffel bag suggests that you are.'

A car swept around her Volvo and sped up the ramp, horn blaring. She took no notice, only kept her serene gaze fixed on Tim.

'Yes, ma'am. All the way to New York.'

'I'll take you to South Carolina – not far into that benighted state, but a little way – if you'll help me out a bit in return. One hand washes the other, if you see what I mean.'

'You scratch my back and I scratch yours,' Tim said, grinning.

'There will be no scratching of any kind, but you may get in.'

Tim did so. Her name was Marjorie Kellerman, and she ran the Brunswick library. She also belonged to something called the Southeastern Library Association. Which, she said, had no money because 'Trump and his cronies took it all back. They understand culture no more than a donkey understands algebra.'

Sixty-five miles north, still in Georgia, she stopped at a pokey little library in the town of Pooler. Tim unloaded the cartons of books and dollied them inside. He dollied another dozen or so cartons out to the Volvo. These, Marjorie Kellerman told him, were bound to the Yemassee Public Library, about forty miles further north, across the

South Carolina state line. But not long after passing Hardeeville, their progress came to a stop. Cars and trucks were stacked up in both lanes, and more quickly filled in behind them.

'Oh, I hate it when this happens,' Marjorie said, 'and it always seems to in South Carolina, where they're too cheap to widen the highway. There's been a wreck somewhere up ahead, and with only two lanes, nobody can get by. I'll be here half the day. Mr Jamieson, you may be excused from further duty. If I were you, I would exit my vehicle, walk back to the Hardeeville exit, and try your luck on Highway 17.'

'What about all those cartons of books?'

'Oh, I'll find another strong back to help me unload,' she said, and smiled at him. 'To tell you the truth, I saw you standing there in the hot sun and just decided to live a little dangerously.'

'Well, if you're sure.' The traffic clog was making him feel claustrophobic. The way he'd felt stuck halfway back in economy class of the Delta flight, in fact. 'If you're not, I'll hang in. It's not like I'm racing a deadline or anything.'

'I'm sure,' she said. 'It's been a pleasure meeting you, Mr Jamieson.'

'Likewise, Ms Kellerman.'

'Do you need monetary assistance? I can spare ten dollars, if you do.'

He was touched and surprised – not for the first time – by the ordinary kindness and generosity of ordinary folks, especially those without much to spare. America was still a good place, no matter how much some (including himself, from time to time) might disagree. 'No, I'm fine. Thank you for the offer.'

He shook her hand, got out, and walked back along the I-95 breakdown lane to the Hardeeville exit. When a ride was not immediately forthcoming on US 17, he strolled a couple of miles to where it joined State Road 92. Here a sign pointed toward the town of DuPray. By then it was late afternoon, and Tim decided he had better find a motel in which to spend the night. It would undoubtedly be another of the cheesedog variety, but the alternatives – sleeping outside and getting eaten alive by skeeters or in some farmer's barn – were even less appealing. And so he set out for DuPray.

Great events turn on small hinges.

4

An hour later he was sitting on a rock at the edge of the two-lane, waiting for a seemingly endless freight train to cross the road. It was headed in the direction of DuPray at a stately thirty miles an hour: boxcars, autoracks (most loaded with wrecks rather than new vehicles), tankers, flatcars, and gondolas loaded with God knew what evil substances that might, in the event of a derailment, catch the piney woods afire or afflict the DuPray populace with noxious or even fatal fumes. At last came an orange caboose where a man in bib overalls sat in a lawn chair, reading a paperback and smoking a cigarette. He looked up from his book and tipped Tim a wave. Tim tipped one right back.

The town was two miles further on, built around the intersection of SR 92 (now called Main Street) and two other streets. DuPray seemed to have largely escaped the chain stores that had taken over the bigger towns; there was a Western Auto, but it was closed down, the windows soaped over. Tim noted a grocery store, a drug store, a mercantile that appeared to sell a little bit of everything, and a couple of beauty salons. There was also a movie theater with FOR SALE OR RENT on the marquee, an auto supply store that fancied itself the DuPray Speed Shop, and a restaurant called Bev's Eatery. There were three churches, one Methodist, two off-brand, all of the come-to-Jesus variety. There were no more than two dozen cars and farm trucks scattered along the slant-parking spaces that lined the business district. The sidewalks were nearly deserted.

Three blocks up, after yet another church, he spied the DuPray Motel. Beyond it, where Main Street presumably reverted to SR 92, there was another rail crossing, a depot, and a row of metal roofs glittering in the sun. Beyond these structures, the piney woods closed in again. All in all, it looked to Tim like a town out of a country ballad, one of those nostalgia pieces sung by Alan Jackson or George Strait. The motel sign was old and rusty, suggesting the place might be as closed-down as the movie theater, but since the afternoon was now ebbing away and it appeared to be the only game in town when it came to shelter, Tim headed for it.

Halfway there, after the DuPray Town Office, he came to a brick building with ladders of ivy climbing the sides. On the neatly mowed lawn was a sign proclaiming this the Fairlee County Sheriff's Department. Tim thought it must be a poor-ass county indeed, if this town was its seat.

Two cruisers were parked in front, one of them a newish sedan, the other an elderly, mud-splashed 4Runner with a bubble light on the dash. Tim looked toward the entrance – the almost unconscious glance of a drifter with quite a lot of cash money in his pocket – walked on a few steps, then turned back for a closer look at the notice boards flanking the double doors. At one of the notices in particular. Thinking he must have read it wrong but wanting to make sure.

Not in this day and age, he thought. Can't be.

But it was. Next to a poster reading IF YOU THOUGHT MARIJUNA IS LEGAL IN SOUTH CAROLINA, **THINK AGAIN**, was one that read simply NIGHT KNOCKER WANTED. APPLY WITHIN.

Wow, he thought. Talk about a blast from the past.

He turned toward the rusty motel sign and paused again, thinking about that help-wanted sign. Just then one of the police station doors opened and a lanky cop came out, settling his cap on his red hair. The latening sun twinkled on his badge. He took in Tim's workboots, dusty jeans, and blue chambray shirt. His eyes dwelled for a moment on the duffel bag slung over Tim's shoulder before moving to his face. 'Can I help you, sir?'

The same impulse that had made him stand up on

the plane swept over him now. 'Probably not, but who knows?'

5

The redheaded cop was Deputy Taggart Faraday. He escorted Tim inside, where the familiar smells of bleach and ammonia cakes wafted into the office from the four-cell holding area in the back. After introducing Tim to Veronica Gibson, the middle-aged deputy working dispatch this afternoon, Faraday asked to see Tim's driver's license and at least one other piece of identification. What Tim produced in addition to his DL was his Sarasota Police ID, making no attempt to hide the fact that it had expired nine months before. Nevertheless, the attitudes of the deputies changed slightly when they saw it.

'You're not a resident of Fairlee County,' Ronnie Gibson said.

'No,' Tim agreed. 'Not at all. But I could be if I got the night knocker job.'

'Doesn't pay much,' Faraday said, 'and in any case it's not up to me. Sheriff Ashworth hires and fires.'

Ronnie Gibson said, 'Our last night knocker retired and moved down to Georgia. Ed Whitlock. He got ALS, that Lou Gehrig's thing. Nice man. Tough break. But he's got people down there to take care of him.'

'It's always the nice ones who get hit with the shit,' Tag Faraday said. 'Give him a form, Ronnie.' Then, to Tim: 'We're a small outfit here, Mr Jamieson, crew of seven and two of them part-time. All the taxpayers can afford. Sheriff John's currently out on patrol. If he's not in by five, five-thirty at the latest, he's gone home to supper and won't be in until tomorrow.'

'I'll be here tonight in any case. Assuming the motel's open, that is.'

'Oh, I think Norbert's got a few rooms,' Ronnie Gibson said. She exchanged a glance with the redhead and they both laughed.

'I'm guessing it might not be a four-star establishment.'

'No comment on that,' Gibson said, 'but I'd check the sheets for those little red bugs before you lie down, if I was you. Why'd you leave Sarasota PD, Mr Jamieson? You're young to retire, I'd say.'

'That's a matter I'll discuss with your chief, assuming he grants me an interview.'

The two officers exchanged another, longer look, then Tag Faraday said, 'Go on and give the man an application, Ronnie. Nice to meet you, sir. Welcome to DuPray. Act right and we'll get along fine.' With that he departed, leaving the alternative to good behavior open to interpretation. Through the barred window, Tim saw the 4Runner back out of its spot and roll off down DuPray's short main street.

The form was on a clipboard. Tim sat down in one of the three chairs against the lefthand wall, placed his duffel between his feet, and began filling it out.

Night knocker, he thought. I will be goddamned.

6

Sheriff Ashworth – Sheriff John to most of the townsfolk as well as to his deputies, Tim discovered – was a big-bellied slow walker. He had basset hound jowls and a lot of white hair. There was a ketchup stain on his uniform shirt. He wore a Glock on his hip and a ruby ring on one pinkie. His accent was strong, his attitude was good-ole-boy friendly, but his eyes, deep in their fatty sockets, were smart and inquisitive. He could have been typecast in one of those southern-cliché movies like *Walking Tall*, if not for the fact that he was black. And something else: a framed certificate of graduation from the FBI's National Academy in Quantico hung on the wall next to the official portrait of President Trump. That was not the sort of thing you got by mailing in cereal boxtops.

'All right, then,' Sheriff John said, rocking back in his office chair. 'I haven't got long. Marcella hates it when I'm late for dinner. Unless there's some sort of crisis, accourse.'

'Understood.'

'So let's get right to the good part. Why'd you leave Sarasota PD and what are you doing here? South Cah'lina doesn't have too many beaten tracks, and DuPray idn't exactly on any of them.'

Ashworth probably wouldn't be on the phone to Sarasota tonight, but he would be in the morning, so there was no point in gilding the lily. Not that Tim wanted to. If he didn't get the night knocker job, he would spend the night in DuPray and move on in the morning, continuing his stop-and-start progress to New York, a journey he now understood to be a necessary hiatus between what had happened one day late last year at Sarasota's Westfield Mall and whatever might happen next. All that aside, honesty was the best policy, if only because lies – especially in an age when almost all information was available to anyone with a keyboard and a Wi-Fi connection – usually came back to haunt the liar.

'I was given a choice between resignation and dismissal. I chose resignation. No one was happy about it, least of all me – I liked my job and I liked the Gulf Coast – but it was the best solution. This way I get a little money, nothing like a full pension, but better than nothing. I split it with my ex-wife.'

'Cause? And make it simple so I can get to my dinner while it's still hot.'

'This won't take long. At the end of my shift one day last November, I swung into the Westfield Mall to buy a pair of shoes. Had to go to a wedding. I was still in uniform, okay?'

'Okay.'

'I was coming out of the Shoe Depot when a woman ran up and said a teenager was waving a gun around up by the movie theater. So I went up there, double-time.'

'Did you draw your weapon?'

'No sir, not then. The kid with the gun was maybe fourteen, and I ascertained that he was either drunk or high. He had another kid down and was kicking him. He was also pointing the gun at him.'

'Sounds like that Cleveland deal. The cop who shot the black kid who was waving a pellet gun.'

'That was in my mind when I approached, but the cop

who shot Tamir Rice swore he thought the kid was waving a real gun around. I was pretty sure the one I saw wasn't real, but I couldn't be *completely* sure. Maybe you know why.'

Sheriff John Ashworth seemed to have forgotten about dinner. 'Because your subject was pointing it at the kid he had on the floor. No sense pointing a fake gun at someone. Unless, I s'pose, the kid on the ground didn't know that.'

'The perp said later he was *shaking* it at the kid, not pointing it. Saying "It's mine, motherfucker, you don't take what's mine." I didn't see that. To me he looked like he was pointing it. I yelled at him to drop the weapon and put his hands up. He either didn't hear me or didn't pay any attention. He just went on kicking and pointing. Or shaking, if that's what he was doing. In any case, I drew my sidearm.' He paused. 'If it makes any difference, these kids were white.'

'Not to me, it doesn't. Kids were fighting. One was down and getting hurt. The other had what might or might not have been a real gun. So did you shoot him? Tell me it didn't come to that.'

'No one got shot. But . . . you know how people will gather around to watch a fistfight, but tend to scatter once a weapon comes out?'

'Sure. If they've got any sense, they run like hell.'

'That happened, except for a few people who stayed even then.'

'The ones filming it with their phones.'

Tim nodded. 'Four or five wannabe Spielbergs. Anyway, I pointed my gun at the ceiling and fired what was supposed to be a warning shot. It might have been a bad decision, but in that moment it seemed like the right one. The only one. There are hanging lights in that part of the mall. The bullet hit one of them and it came down dead-center on a lookie-loo's head. The kid with the gun dropped it, and as soon as it hit the floor, I knew for sure it wasn't real because it bounced. Turned out to be a plastic squirt gun made to look like a .45 auto. The kid who was on the floor getting kicked had some bruises and a few cuts, nothing that looked like it would need stitches, but the bystander was unconscious and stayed that way for three hours. Concussion. According to his lawyer he's got amnesia and blinding headaches.'

'Sued the department?'

'Yes. It'll go on for awhile, but he'll end up getting something.'

Sheriff John considered. 'If he hung around to film the altercation, he may not get all that much, no matter how bad his headaches are. I suppose the department landed you with reckless discharge of a weapon.'

They had, and it would be nice, Tim thought, if we could leave it at that. But they couldn't. Sheriff John might look like an African-American version of Boss Hogg in *The Dukes of Hazzard*, but he was no dummy. He was clearly sympathetic to Tim's situation – almost any cop would be – but he'd still check. Better he got the rest of the story from Tim himself.

'Before I went into the shoe store, I went into Beachcombers and had a couple of drinks. The responding officers who took the kid into custody smelled it on my breath and gave me the test. I blew oh-six, under the legal limit but not good considering I had just fired my sidearm and put a man in the hospital.'

'You ordinarily a drinking man, Mr Jamieson?'

'Quite a lot in the six months or so after my divorce, but that was two years ago. Not now.' Which is, of course, what I *would* say, he thought.

'Uh-huh, uh-huh, now let's see if I got this right.' The sheriff stuck up a fat index finger. 'You were off duty, which means if you'd been out of uniform, that woman never would have run up to you in the first place.'

'Probably not, but I would have heard the commotion

and gone to the scene anyway. A cop is never really off duty. As I'm sure you know.'

'Uh-huh, uh-huh, but would you have had your gun?'

'No, it would have been locked in my car.'

Ashworth popped a second finger for that point, then added a third. 'The kid had what was probably a fake gun, but it could have been real. You couldn't be sure, one way or the other.'

'Yes.'

Here came finger number four. 'Your warning shot struck a light, not only bringing it down but bringing it down on an innocent bystander's head. If, that is, you can call an asshole filming with a cell phone an innocent bystander.'

Tim nodded.

Up popped the sheriff's thumb. 'And before this alter-cation occurred, you just happened to have ingested two alcoholic drinks.'

'Yes. And while I was in uniform.'

'Not a good decision, not a good . . . what do they call it . . . *optic*, but I'd still have to say you had one insane run of bad luck.' Sheriff John drummed his fingers on the edge of his desk. The ruby pinkie ring punctuated each roll with a small click. 'I think your story is too outrageous not to be true, but I believe I'll call your previous place of employment and check it for myself. If for no other reason than to hear the story again and marvel anew.'

Tim smiled. 'I reported to Bernadette DiPino. She's the Sarasota Chief of Police. And you better get home to dinner, or your wife is going to be mad.'

'Uh-huh, uh-huh, you let me worry about Marcy.' The sheriff leaned forward over his stomach. His eyes were brighter than ever. 'If I Breathalyzed you right now, Mr Jamieson, what would you blow?'

'Go ahead and find out.'

'Don't believe I will. Don't believe I need to.' He leaned back; his office chair uttered another longsuffering squall. 'Why would you want the job of night knocker in a pissant little burg like this? It only pays a hundred dollars a week, and while it doesn't amount to much in the way of trouble Sunday to Thursday, it can be an aggravation on Friday and Saturday nights. The strip club in Penley closed down last year, but there are several ginmills and juke joints in the immediate area.'

'My grandfather was a night knocker in Hibbing, Minnesota. The town where Bob Dylan grew up? This was after he retired from the State Police. He was the reason I wanted to be a cop when I was growing up. I saw the sign, and just thought . . .' Tim shrugged. What *had* he thought? Pretty much the same thing as when he'd taken the job in the recycling plant. A whole lot of nothing much. It occurred to him that he might be, mentally speaking, at least, in sort of a hard place.

'Following in your grandpop's footsteps, uh-huh.' Sheriff John clasped his hands over his considerable belly and stared at Tim – those bright, inquisitive eyes deep in their pockets of fat. 'Consider yourself retired, is that the deal? Just looking for something to while away the idle hours? A little young for that, wouldn't you say?'

'Retired from the police, yes. That's over. A friend said he could get me security work in New York, and I wanted a change of scene. Maybe I don't have to go to New York to get one.' He guessed what he really wanted was a change of heart. The night knocker job might not accomplish that, but then again it might.

'Divorced, you say?'

'Yes.'

'Kids?'

'No. She wanted them, I didn't. Didn't feel I was ready.'

Sheriff John looked down at Tim's application. 'It says here you're forty-two. In most cases – probably not all – if you're not ready by then . . .'

He trailed off, waiting in best cop fashion for Tim to fill the silence. Tim didn't.

'You may be headed to New York eventually, Mr Jamieson, but right now you're just drifting. That fair to say?'

Tim thought it over and agreed it *was* fair.

'If I give you this job, how do I know you won't take a notion to just drift on out of here two weeks or a month from now? DuPray idn't the most interesting place on earth, or even in South Cah'lina. What I'm asking, sir, is how do I know you're dependable?'

'I'll stick around. Always assuming you feel like I'm doing the job, that is. If you decide I'm not, you'll can me. If I should decide to move on, I'll give you plenty of notice. That's a promise.'

'Job's not enough to live on.'

Tim shrugged. 'I'll find something else if I need to. You want to tell me I'd be the only guy around here working two jobs to make ends meet? And I've got a little put by to get started on.'

Sheriff John sat where he was for a little while, thinking it over, then got to his feet. He did it with surprising agility for such a heavy man. 'You come around tomorrow morning and we'll see what we're gonna do about this. Around ten would be about right.'

Which will give you plenty of time to talk to Sarasota PD, Tim thought, and see if my story checks out. Also to discover if there are other smudges on my record.

He stood himself and stuck out his hand. Sheriff John's grip was a good strong one. 'Where will you be staying tonight, Mr Jamieson?'

'That motel down the way, if there's a vacant room.'

'Oh, Norbert'll have plenty of vacant rooms,' the sheriff said, 'and I doubt if he'll try to sell you any of the herb. You've still got a little of the cop look about you, seems to me. If you don't have a problem digesting fried food, Bev's down the street is open until seven. I'm partial to the liver and onions, myself.'

'Thanks. And thanks for talking to me.'

'Not at all. Interesting conversation. And when you check in at the DuPray, tell Norbert Sheriff John said to give you one of the good rooms.'

'I'll do that.'

'But I'd still take a look for bugs before you climb into the rack.'

Tim smiled. 'I already got that advice.'

7

Dinner at Bev's Eatery was chicken-fried steak, green beans, and peach cobbler to follow. Not bad. The room he was assigned at the DuPray Motel was a different matter. It made the ones Tim had stayed in during his ramble north look like palaces. The air conditioner in the window rattled busily, but didn't cool things off much. The rusty shower head dripped, and there seemed to be no way to stop it. (He finally put a towel under it to muffle the clockwork sound.) The shade on the bedside lamp was burned in a couple of places. The room's one picture – an unsettling composition depicting a sailing ship crewed entirely by grinning and possibly homicidal black men – hung crooked. Tim straightened it, but it immediately fell crooked again.

There was a lawn chair outside. The seat sagged and the legs were as rusty as the defective shower head, but it held him. He sat there with his legs stretched out, slapping at bugs and watching the sun burn its orange furnace light through the trees. Looking at it made him feel happy and melancholy at the same time. Another nearly endless freight appeared around quarter past eight, rolling across the state road and past the warehouses on the outskirts of town.

'That damn Georgia Southern's always late.'

Tim looked around and beheld the proprietor and sole evening employee of this fine establishment. He was rail thin. A paisley vest hung off his top half. He wore his khakis high-water, the better to display his white socks and elderly Converse sneakers. His vaguely ratlike face was framed by a vintage Beatle haircut.

'Do tell,' Tim said.

'Doesn't matter,' Norbert said, shrugging. 'The even' train always goes right through. The midnight train *most* always does unless it's got diesel to unload or fresh fruit n vegimals for the grocery. There's a junction down yonder.' He crossed his index fingers to demonstrate. 'The one line goes to Atlanta, Birmin'am, Huntsville, places like 'at. T'other comes up from Jacksonville and goes on to Charleston, Wilmington, Newport News, places like 'at. It's the day freights that mostly stop. Y'all thinkin about warehouse work? They usually a man or two short over there. Got to have a strong back, though. Not for me.'

Tim looked at him. Norbert shuffled his sneakers and gave a grin that exposed what Tim thought of as gone-country teeth. They were there, but looked as if they might be gone soon.

'Where's your car?'

Tim just kept looking.

'Are you a cop?'

'Just now I'm a man watching the sun go down through the trees,' Tim said, 'and I would as soon do it alone.'

'Say nummore, say nummore,' Norbert said, and beat a retreat, pausing only for a single narrow, assessing glance over his shoulder.

The freight eventually passed. The red crossing lights quit. The barriers swung up. The two or three vehicles that had been waiting started their engines and got moving. Tim watched the sun go from orange to red as it sank — *red sky at night, sailor's delight*, his night knocker gramp would have said. He watched the shadows of the pines lengthen across SR 92 and join together. He was quite sure he wasn't going to get the night knocker job, and maybe that was for the best. DuPray felt far from everything, not just a sidetrack but a damn near no-track. If not for those four warehouses, the town probably wouldn't exist. And what was the *point* of their existence? To store TVs from some northern port like Wilmington or Norfolk, so they could eventually be shipped on to Atlanta or Marietta? To store boxes of computer supplies shipped from Atlanta so they could eventually be loaded up again and shipped to Wilmington or Norfolk or Jacksonville? To store fertilizer or dangerous chemicals, because in this part of the United States there was no law against it? Around and around it went, and what was round *had* no point, any fool knew that.

He went inside, locked his door (stupid; the thing was so flimsy a single kick would stave it in), shucked down to his underwear, and lay on the bed, which was saggy but bugless (as far as he had been able to ascertain, at least). He put his hands behind his head and stared at the picture of the grinning black men manning the frigate or whatever the hell you called a ship like that. Where were they going? Were they pirates? They looked like pirates to him. Whatever they were, it would eventually come to loading and unloading at the next port of call. Maybe everything did. And everyone. Not long ago he had unloaded himself from a Delta flight bound for New York. After that he had loaded cans and bottles into a sorting machine. Today he had loaded books for a nice lady librarian at one place and unloaded them at another. He was only here because I-95 had loaded up with cars and trucks waiting for the wreckers to come and haul away some unfortunate's crashed car. Probably after an ambulance had loaded up the driver and unloaded him at the nearest hospital.

But a night knocker doesn't load or unload, Tim

thought. He just walks and knocks. That is, Grandpa would have said, the beauty part.

He fell asleep, waking only at midnight, when another freight went rumbling through. He used the bathroom and, before going back to bed, took down the crooked picture and leaned the crew of grinning black men facing the wall.

Damn thing gave him the willies.

**Love Castle Rock? Don't miss
GWENDY'S BUTTON BOX by Stephen King and
Richard Chizmar**

**The small town of Castle Rock has witnessed some
strange events and unusual visitors over the years, but
there is one story that has never been told . . . until now.**

There are three ways up to Castle View from the town of Castle
Rock: Route 117, Pleasant Road, and the Suicide Stairs. Every
day in the summer of 1974 twelve-year-old Gwendy Peterson
takes the stairs, which are held by strong (if time-rusted) iron
bolts and zig-zag up the cliffside.

One day, while Gwendy catches her breath and listens to the
shouts of the kids on the playground and the chink of an
aluminium bat hitting a baseball, a stranger calls out to her.

On a bench in the shade sits a man in a small, neat black hat.
He offers Gwendy a mahogany box with coloured buttons.
The buttons will produce gifts, such as chocolate which can
make you slimmer. But he warns her that the gifts will be
'small recompense for the responsibility'.

'Man, I love this story! The whole thing just races and feels so
right-sized and so scarily and sadly relevant. Loved the characters
. . . and the sense of one little girl's connection to the whole world
through this weird device. It all just sang' – J.J. Abrams

'A resonant novella set in one of King's signature locales: the
small town of Castle Rock, Maine' – Washington Post

HODDER

Look out for GWENDY'S MAGIC FEATHER
By Richard Chizmar

Prepare to return again to Stephen King's Castle Rock, the sleepy little town built on a bedrock of deep, dark secrets, which is about to awaken from its quiet slumber once more.

In Washington DC, thirty-seven-year-old Gwendy Peterson could not be more different from the girl who climbed the Suicide Stairs.

Gwendy has never told a soul about the button box – not even her husband. But one day the button box shows up without warning and without the man in the black suit to explain what she is supposed to do with it. The curious reappearance of the box, along with the troubling disappearances in Castle Rock, leads Gwendy home again . . . where she just might be able to help rescue the missing girls and stop a dangerous man before he does something too terrible to contemplate . . .

'In the story you're about to read – lucky you! – all of Rich's formidable skills are on display. He evokes Castle Rock well, and the regular Joes and regular Jills that populate the town ring true. We know these people, and so we care for them. We also care for Gwendy. To tell you the truth, I sort of fell in love with her, and I'm delighted that she's back for more.'
– Stephen King (from his foreword)

HODDER &
STOUGHTON

Discover DOCTOR SLEEP by Stephen King
A major movie from October 2019

Following a childhood haunted by terrifying events at the
Overlook Hotel, Dan Torrance has been drifting for decades.
Finally, he settles into a job at a nursing home where he draws
on his remnant 'shining' power to provide crucial comfort to the
dying. Aided by a prescient cat, he becomes 'Doctor Sleep'.

Then he meets Abra Stone, a girl with the brightest 'shining'
ever seen. But her gift is attracting the beautiful yet merciless
Rose the Hat and her followers, the True Knot. They may look
harmless, the sort of people who are devoted to their campers
and RVs, but in their twisted quest for immortality they live off
the 'steam' that children like Abra produce.

Now Dan must call upon his powers once more as he battles for
Abra's soul and survival – facing his fears and reawakening ghosts
from his past.

'Sheer page-turning suspense . . . addictive . . . a triumph from
the world's finest horror novelist' – *Sunday Express*

'By the end of this book your fingers will be mere stubs of their
former selves . . . King's inventiveness and skill show no signs of
slacking. *Doctor Sleep* has all the virtues of his best work'
– Margaret Atwood, *New York Times*

HODDER

Stay awake with THE SHINING by Stephen King

**Before DOCTOR SLEEP, there was THE SHINING,
a classic of modern American horror from the
undisputed master, Stephen King.**

Danny is only five years old, but in the words of old Mr
Hallorann he is a 'shiner', aglow with psychic voltage. When his
father becomes caretaker of the Overlook Hotel, Danny's visions
grow out of control.

As winter closes in and blizzards cut them off, the hotel seems to
develop a life of its own. It is meant to be empty. So who is the
lady in Room 217 and who are the masked guests going up and
down in the elevator? And why do the hedges shaped like
animals seem so alive?

Somewhere, somehow, there is an evil force in the hotel – and
that, too, is beginning to shine . . .

'Obviously a masterpiece, probably the best supernatural novel
in a hundred years' – Peter Straub

HODDER

To find out more about Stephen King
please visit www.hodder.co.uk,
www.stephenkingbooks.co.uk,
www.facebook.com/stephenkingbooks